"How long do you plan to be here?"

"The audition is in six weeks. Meanwhile, I'm staying at a friend's cabin."

Six weeks?

Gloom hung over his shoulders like a sweaty gym towel. An *actress* at his center.

"Of course, if things go well, I could leave earlier."

Mandy entered the room and handed her a volunteer packet. "Take this home and read through it. It lays out all the jobs you'd be doing."

Tim cleared his throat as the words he was about to say stuck in his craw. "If you decide to fill out the volunteer application, I'll be hap. . .I'll do what I can to help." If he could step up the training, he might be able to have her out of there in half that time.

She perused the stapled stack of printed paper. "Thank you. Vic offered, too."

That bothered him. Vic would no doubt do more flirting than actual training and stall the process.

"You should take Tim up on his offer," Mandy said, unwittingly helping his cause. "He's also a falconer, the best I've ever seen."

"Then you're my man." The actress flashed a brilliant smile.

Tim wanted to do his own running and screaming. What had he done?

KATHLEEN E. KOVACH and her husband, Jim, raised two sons while living the nomadic lifestyle for over twenty years in the Air Force. She's a grandmother, though much too young for that. Now firmly planted in Colorado, she's a member of American Christian Fiction Writers and leads a local writers group. Kathleen hopes her readers will giggle through her books while learning the spiritual truths God has placed there. Visit her Web site at www.kathleenekovach.com.

Books by Kathleen E. Kovach

HEARTSONG PRESENTS
HP717—Merely Players
HP870—God Gave the Song
HP894—Crossroads Bay

Fine, Feathered Friend

Kathleen E. Kovach

Heartsong Presents

To Jim, who, through his love, helps me spread my wings and soar.

I would like to thank my mother, Ruth Keal; my sister, Shari Warren; and my brother-in-law, Neil Warren, for all their help as they escorted me throughout Oregon and answered my incessant questions. To my awesome crit group who keeps me grounded, you all are the best. And to the Cascades Raptor Center in Eugene, Oregon, many thanks for the tour.

A note from the Author:
I love to hear from my readers! You may correspond with me by writing:

Kathleen E. Kovach
Author Relations
PO Box 721
Uhrichsville, OH 44683

ISBN 978-1-60260-963-1

FINE, FEATHERED FRIEND

Scripture taken from the HOLY BIBLE, NEW INTERNATIONAL VERSION®. NIV®. Copyright © 1973, 1978, 1984 by International Bible Society. Used by permission of Zondervan. All rights reserved.

All of the characters and events in this book are fictitious. Any resemblance to actual persons, living or dead, or to actual events is purely coincidental.

Our mission is to publish and distribute inspirational products offering exceptional value and biblical encouragement to the masses.

PRINTED IN THE U.S.A.

"I can't do this." Glenys gripped her cell phone with a sweaty palm while glancing back with longing at her rental car in the parking lot.

"Yes you can." Trista's voice reached her through the receiver and past the fear-induced buzzing in her ears. Her best friend spoke with a mixture of exasperation and encouragement.

"But there are birds in there. And not just birds. Big birds. Predators. Eagles." She swallowed hard. "Falcons."

The gate gaped before her, its teethlike spiked fence posts looking more like a fort than a bird sanctuary. She felt safer on the outside.

"I should have come with you." Trista sighed. "How badly do you want the movie role?"

Glenys squeezed her phone until she expected her friend on the other end to gasp for air. "Bad enough to fly here to Oregon and leave you in Los Angeles."

"That's not bad enough, although I do miss you."

"Okay, so badly that I've already written my Oscar acceptance speech."

"Well, I think Oscar is a little ambitious since this is a minor role. But I think you've proven you want it at all costs."

"The part is totally mine if I can just get over this fear." And moving past the sign that read SHADY PINE RAPTOR CENTER would be the first step to conquering that fear.

A crisp breeze signaling an early autumn whispered through the Douglas fir that hugged the hillside. Even so, Glenys broke into a nervous sweat under her rabbit fur–collared suede jacket.

"All you have to do is hold a falcon."

"I know." Why did the most promising movie role to come along ever in her career have to involve falcon handling? "By the way, have I thanked you for letting me stay at your cabin?"

"No, but I figured you were stressed." Trista laughed, and Glenys could imagine her tossing her dark waves with a flip of her hand. "I'm just happy I could suggest it. It's been in my family for years."

"Well, I'm grateful. The nearest raptor center to me was a seven-hour drive away. Kinda far for a day trip."

"No problem. Now, you can do this. Put one foot in front of the other. All the birds are in cages. And there are professionals in there who will be sure you're safe."

"You're right. I'm just being silly."

"No, not silly. Phobias are real—I know that. I'm still a little afraid of the dark."

Glenys closed her eyes and focused on her friend. She prayed that Trista would embrace the Lord and be redeemed from an eternity of darkness. Thinking of someone else loosened her feet to take one more step.

Trista sighed. "But we all have to make sacrifices in this business."

Here it comes. Trista had made it successfully in Hollywood with minimal sacrifice thanks to her daddy, Anthony Farentino, the successful producer who had helped launch a galaxy of movie stars. Yet she had no problem spouting advice to those who struggled with their craft.

"*Some* of us have had to make sacrifices, Little Miss Director's Daughter." Glenys and Trista often bantered on this subject. But Glenys made her tone light to make it known she was only kidding, although there was much truth in it.

"Hey, don't knock it. If it weren't for Dad, you wouldn't even be up for this role."

It was true. She had auditioned for Mr. Farentino in other

projects, but for this one he had actually approached her, insisting she would be perfect for the role of falcon handler. How could she turn that down?

And now she stood outside a bird sanctuary that nursed injured and ill predatory birds—facing her largest fear.

"Have you moved yet?" Trista's voice held an impatient tone.

"No."

"I don't know what else to do for you then. I was hoping you could talk to someone with a passion for raptors. Maybe then you'd see they aren't so scary. And remember, there's only one scene in the movie where you have to actually hold one. Surely you can do that."

"I know. You've been a great friend through all of this. I'm just being a big baby."

A bubbling giggle in the receiver assured Glenys that Trista still loved her. "Hey, I'm just concerned you'll miss this opportunity. Consider my nudging a thank-you for holding my hand during the stalker scare. You and your dad really came through for me."

Another reason Glenys hated predators. Stalkers came with and without feathers.

"How is the judge, anyway?" Trista asked. "I haven't seen his name in the news lately."

Glenys laughed. "Laying low, thanks to you. I don't think he appreciates being labeled 'Judge to the Stars.'"

"Listen, I've got to go. Please promise me you'll give this a chance. I know it will work. You might pray to that God of yours. Doesn't He have a thing about fear?"

" 'Fear of man' "—*and birds*—" 'will prove to be a snare, but whoever trusts in the LORD is kept safe.' From Proverbs 29:25. I quoted it to you when you had to face your stalker."

"I remember."

Glenys sent a quick praise that the seed seemed to have burrowed somewhere in Trista's heart.

The two fell silent for a moment. Finally, to prove to Trista she practiced what she preached, Glenys took a step. "I'm moving."

"Forward?"

"Yes." Glenys allowed a tinge of irritation in the word, but knew the validity of Trista's question.

"Great! Keep those feet going, and report back to me this evening. I'm proud of you, Glen!"

Trista hung up, and Glenys's feet stopped with the silence. She continued to grip the phone—her only connection to sanity. No, that wasn't correct. God was her connection, and she repeated the verse on fear for herself and added, *I can do everything through Him who gives me strength.* Then she moved past the wooden sign and nearer to the sounds of screeching, cawing, and flapping feathers.

A school bus had pulled into the parking lot while Glenys was on the phone, and now four dozen seven-year-olds flocked by her, all doing their own squawking and twittering. The children and a handful of adults had smiles on their faces, as if they were actually happy to be near talons and sharp beaks.

She followed along, swept into their wake, more secure tagging behind the crowd. If something was going to attack, she had a solid human barrier.

No, Glenys, God does not condone sacrificing children. Well, maybe they'd make enough noise to keep any stray predators away.

They walked up a short hill to a log building. A rustic sign, basically a board nailed to a stake in the ground, pointed the way to the visitor center. She decided to duck in there while a member of the staff greeted the kids and laid out the game plan to the chaperones.

Gingerly opening the squeaky door, she entered a small room cluttered with brochures, promotional material, and children's educational pages to take home. There were also knickknacks, coloring books, small toys, and other items to buy. The inside reflected the rustic outside with its rough-hewn wood-plank walls. But those were hard to see for all the shelves of books and posters of birds on the walls.

"May I help you, sweetheart?"

The voice sounded like an elderly woman. She searched the room. No one was there. A slight flap of feathers to her left caught her eye. In the corner a large gray parrot sat on a perch and watched her intently with creepy yellow eyes.

Glenys froze. Why wasn't the creature in a cage?

The bird tilted its head and opened its beak. "May I help you, sweetheart?"

She clutched her chest where her heartbeat threatened to break through the skin. As she tore the door open with a vow on her lips to give up acting and take up snake charming, a male voice stopped her.

"May I help you?"

She turned slowly to see a man, probably in his thirties, tilting his head in the same way the parrot had. His sandy-brown shaggy hair fell into his eyes, and he swept it away with mild annoyance. By the eagle logo on his khaki shirt breast pocket, she gathered that he worked at the center.

As she leaned against the door, it closed with a click, but the doorknob became her symbolic safe place, and she curled the fingers of her left hand around it even tighter as she eyed the gray reaper in the corner.

"Um. . .I'm here to look at birds."

A smile tugged at his cheek, and she noticed his eyes for the first time. Brown with a twinkle of gold.

"Well, you've come to the right place."

"Right place, *awk!*"

Glenys jumped slightly. *Get a grip. It's just a silly parrot.*

"And here's your first opportunity." He walked over to the

parrot and held out his hand. The bird hopped on and sidled upward to his shoulder. From there it scrutinized Glenys as if it were about to ask for her credentials. She shrank farther into the closed wooden door, her hand still on the doorknob behind her back. The man seemed to notice her consternation and kept his distance.

"This is Cyrano. Say hello, Cyrano."

"*Awk.* Come here, sweetheart."

The man rolled his eyes. "Sorry for his manners. He's influenced by too many people here." He fed Cyrano a sunflower seed he'd pulled from his pocket, then touched his chest. "I'm Tim Vogel, bird handler."

Glenys would have extended her hand, but didn't trust the parrot's sharp beak. "Glenys Bernard, actress. I'm here on a research mission."

Instead of the usual interest people would exhibit when she'd tell them her profession, Tim's eyes dulled noticeably. Then they shifted away as he placed Cyrano back on his perch.

Before she could ask why there was a tropical bird at a raptor center, someone opened the door, with difficulty since Glenys was still holding on to the doorknob. A woman poked her head in, bumping the door into Glenys's backside. "Oh, excuse me! Tim, they're ready for you."

"Okay, I'll be right there." He glanced at Glenys. "I'm giving a tour to those kids out there."

Glenys didn't want to be left alone with even a social bird like Cyrano. "May I tag along? I'll probably learn more in a group than by taking a self-guided tour."

His eyes darted to the doorknob. "Of course, but you're going to have to let go."

She released the knob quickly, as if it had turned into a hot charcoal briquette. He motioned with his hand for her to go ahead, but the friendly smile had dissolved into a thin brooding line—and ice had entered the room.

❧

Tim followed the skittish woman to join Mandy and the students waiting for a day of raptor education. Ironic that an actress would walk into his sanctuary on the very day he received a cell phone text from his mother detailing why she couldn't visit—again. He couldn't decide if she was just in denial over Gramps's mental condition or if she simply didn't care about them anymore. It had been a couple of years since she tore herself from Hollywood and her stagnant career as an actress.

Mandy introduced him to the energetic group. He tried to forget about his mom, and actresses in general, because right now, at this moment, nothing mattered except sharing his passion with young bird enthusiasts.

"Hi, guys! You ready to learn about some awesome birds?"

"Yeah!" they shouted, which is what he knew they'd do.

"Then you'll have to do me a favor. This area here is the only place you can be noisy and run around, okay?" He leaned against one of the four picnic tables and gestured with his arms to show the craft area in which they were standing. "This is a bird hospital as well as a nature center, and some of our patients need their rest. So if it starts to get a little noisy, I'll just do this." He put his finger on his lips. "Then you all do the same, and when it's quiet I'll continue with the tour. Deal?"

"Deal!"

Tim laughed at their enthusiasm. At this impressionable age, he hoped most of them would come away with a new respect for the raptor. And maybe one or two would dedicate their lives to preserving the species. Which is what had happened to him during a field trip when he was ten.

He continued to address the group. "Okay, half of you are going to stay here for now and do a fun craft project with Miss Mandy, the center's director. The rest will follow me up the hill, and I'll introduce you to some of my friends."

The groups split off, and as he began the trek up the gentle slope to the large enclosures, he noticed the actress hanging behind. Was she contemplating doing crafts with the kids? However, she eventually trailed the group and was the last to join them as they gathered at the first enclosure. A little girl asked her if she was someone's mom.

"No, I came to see the birds, just like you. May I join you?"

The little girl in red pigtails nodded. "You can be my mom. She couldn't make it today."

The actress smiled, showing an intriguing dimple. "Thank you."

Tim waited until he had everyone's attention. "This first bird is a red-tailed hawk. Her name is Heidi." Heidi watched the children from a branch. "Who can tell me what hawks eat?"

Hands shot up, but they still called out their ideas.

"Bugs!"

"Lizards!"

"Dead stuff!"

"Actually, hawks hunt for live food. Farmers love hawks because they help rid them of grasshoppers, gophers, rabbits, and mice."

The actress went just a touch pale and reached out to hold the red-headed girl's hand.

Tim continued. "But Heidi can't do that right now because she was shot with a BB gun and has nerve damage to her wing."

"What do you do with birds who can't be released?" a teacher asked.

"We try to find a good home in a zoo or other place specifically designed for wildlife, but if there is none available, we keep them for educational purposes, which is what I'm doing right now." He left out the third option, euthanasia. "In any case, we must be very careful with our feathered friends and not shoot at them, right?"

"Right!"

"Now, since Heidi can't hunt for herself,"—he rummaged in his sweatshirt pocket—"I need to feed her." He drew out a feathered carcass. "This is a our version of pizza delivery, only it's quail."

"Ew!" The kids spoke collectively, but the grins and mock-disgusted faces proved they weren't scarred for life.

He quickly replaced the dead bird into his sweatshirt pocket and turned to unlock the screened wooden door. "All of our enclosures have two doors. Double security to keep our birds in."

The actress raised her hand. "Excuse me. Have they ever gotten out?"

Tim shook his head. "Not since I've been here." He continued to walk into the enclosure and grabbed a gauntlet from the hook near the inner door. "Notice how I approach her. I never make her do anything she doesn't want to." He used his soft voice as he pulled on the glove. "Hey, you want to meet some kids?" He offered his arm, and Heidi stepped onto his hand. He held up a length of leather. "I use this leash to clip onto the leather straps attached to the anklets on her legs. These straps are called jesses." He demonstrated by clipping the leash into the ring at the joined jesses nine inches from her body. Then he wrapped the jesses and leash around his palm. "This helps me keep a tight rein on her so she won't fly away." When he brought Heidi out, he noticed that the actress had backed several yards away. Yep. Fear of birds.

The kids continued to ask questions while he tried to get the hawk to take the carcass from his hand, but she was too busy watching the crowd—specifically the actress, who, even though she'd backed away significantly, was still within Heidi's excellent field of vision.

Oh man! Why hadn't he noticed? She had a fur collar on her jacket. Heidi must have thought it was a rodent. Her gaze zoned in as if she were about to swoop onto her prey, and she flapped for all she was worth. Thankfully, Tim had a good hold on her, but he felt her strength.

"Shh. Settle down." Heidi tucked her wings back in as she lost interest in her target, who was now running down the hill, punching the numbers on her cell phone, and screaming as if she were in an Alfred Hitchcock movie.

two

"I can't do this!"

Glenys shrieked into her phone at Trista's voice mail. She snapped the cover closed as the hysteria threatened to collapse her chest.

"Miss!" The voice called to her from behind before she could reach the safety of her car. Glenys turned to see the short, stocky woman called Mandy chasing her down. When she caught up to her, she gathered her long brown-gray hair over one shoulder and wheezed, "Tim called me on the radio." She indicated the black box in her hand. "He was concerned something had upset you."

"That *something* was one of your birds. It lunged at me." A breeze flipped the fur collar on her jacket, tickling her chin.

Mandy's gaze honed in on Glenys's neck, and Glenys feared the woman would flap a feather and lunge, too.

"You might want to take off your jacket." Mandy pointed to the collar. "The hawk probably thought it was alive."

Glenys ripped the garment from her body and balled the collar inside while searching the sky for other predators. "That bird could have slashed an artery going for my clothing."

"You poor dear. How close were you to it?" Mandy's concern touched Glenys.

She glanced around. "About as far as we are to my car."

Mandy took in the several yards of gravel, then looked perplexed. "That far away?"

"Well, it seemed much closer at the time."

Mandy touched her arm. "I recognize the signs. You have a fear of birds."

15

"Yes, especially predatory birds."

"Me, too."

Glenys couldn't believe that. "How can you work here?"

Mandy laughed while pulling Glenys to a park bench near the center's entrance. "Maybe I should have said that I'm a recovering ornithophobiac. It's why I initially wanted to volunteer here. Now I'm the director."

Glenys looked around at the rustic area. "You did this to yourself?"

She nodded. "Are you willing to come back in? I need to return to the school kids, but I'd love to tell you how I got over my fear."

Glenys hesitated. How much did she want the movie role? She'd been playing in indie films and obscure roles in commercials for too long. She not only wanted this role, but she also needed this role.

Mandy flashed a compassionate smile.

Everything inside Glenys said to run and not look back. But this woman's kindness drew her past the gaping teethlike spikes and back into her nightmare.

While walking, Glenys unbuttoned the collar from her jacket and jammed it into her purse. Then she pulled the sleeves back over her arms before the crisp air could produce goose bumps.

They entered the craft area where she sat at a picnic table with the kids, Mandy lowering herself next to her.

One of the boys passed her a fist-sized pinecone. "We're making owls."

"Okay." Apparently she had no choice but to craft. "So," she asked Mandy while sticking a piece of prepared poster board cut like a wing into the pinecone, "how did you overcome?"

"I met a guy I really liked. He was into hiking, camping, and outdoorsy stuff. I've been allergic to the outdoors all my life." She smiled. "I grew up in Seattle in an apartment. My family was artsy. We went to plays, art expos, operas." She passed the glue to a parent. "When I met Jason, our first date was an overnight biking trip with a group of friends at Mount Rainier. I knew I was skittish around anything with feathers, but when the camp robbers—beautiful but pesky blue jays—attacked the food on our picnic table, I freaked." She stopped to encourage a ponytailed girl across the table, then turned her attention back to Glenys. "Not only did I realize how afraid I was of birds, but I also learned that weekend I was afraid of bugs, flying campfire embers, and high places. Basically, I was afraid of nature."

"Maybe I should be calling *you* 'poor dear'!"

"Oh, I was afraid of the deer, too. I'd never seen one in the wild. It walked right into our camp."

"I'm guessing your guy is very patient."

"He must be because he married me twenty years ago." She laughed. "We both had to go through a patience phase early in our relationship. But I realized he was worth keeping, so I knew I had to get over some of my phobias if I wanted to keep him in my life. He's the one who suggested I volunteer here, and I'm not going to lie to you, it was hard at first. But once I got to know the birds and learned how to handle them, I started to feel comfortable. When the director position opened up, my past work experience met the criteria, so I snapped it up. And now I can't imagine doing anything else."

Glenys considered her words. "How are you at bugs and campfire embers?"

"I still hate bugs, but I'm getting better at campfires. On my next birthday, I'm tackling another phobia with my man— skydiving. Try that with a fear of heights!"

"Will you need prayer?"

"I'm sure I will!"

Glenys had just finished a wise old pinecone owl when a door opened on a building marked CLINIC. A tall man sporting a thin black mustache sauntered toward them.

"Hey, sweetheart." He winked at Mandy. "How's it going?"

Mandy rolled her eyes. "Fine. You want to make an owl?"

Glenys lowered her voice. "Is that your man?"

Mandy belly-laughed. "No way. But Vic thinks he is, just as he thinks all the women who work here belong to him."

Glenys could tell Vic was a tad overconfident. After raking her with a glance, he strutted like a rooster in a henhouse as he showed off for the three mom chaperones. They giggled, which only fueled his flirting.

Then he looked back at Glenys and made an obvious note of her ringless finger.

He sauntered over to the picnic table and gently grasped the shoulders of the little boy who had been sitting next to her, sliding him aside.

The boy protested. "Hey!"

Plopping down onto the now-vacant space, Vic spoke out of the side of his mouth. "Great owl, kid."

"Thanks." That seemed to appease the child.

He turned his back on him and concentrated on Glenys. "Haven't I seen you somewhere before?"

Seriously? Did he get that pickup line from the book *Bad Clichés and When to Use Them*? Glenys wished she could slide in the opposite direction, but Mandy blocked her.

He continued to scrutinize her. "Are you a teacher?"

"No."

Clueless, Mandy introduced the two. "Vic, this is Glenys. Tim told me on the walkie-talkie that she's an actress. Just came here on her own and joined the kids."

He shook a pointed finger. "I know where I've seen you. That insurance commercial."

"Wow." Glenys was never recognized in her work. "You're right. I was an extra in the background talking to an agent while the spokesperson did his spiel. How did you identify me?"

"I never forget a pretty face."

Mandy fake-coughed and telegraphed a message with her eyes to Glenys that said, *See? God's gift to women.* Then she said, "It's pretty cool that you're an actress. I could never do that."

"Something else to overcome? You could join a community theater."

"One phobia at a time, thank you very much."

"So." Vic claimed her attention again. "What brings you here on your own?"

"I'm researching a movie role."

"Really?" His eyebrows shot up as he leaned in, clearly interested. She was suddenly drawn to this charismatic man, despite his flirting. But she knew to keep her distance. Hollywood was full of guys like Vic.

"The character I would be playing is a falcon handler. Since I have no experience with birds, I thought I would visit and get some, firsthand. But I'm slightly skittish of birds. So I have a challenge to overcome before the role is mine."

"Hey"—Mandy motioned toward the trail—"Tim could help with that. He's a falconer."

"He's busy." Vic dismissed the idea. "But I have some time. Let me show you around."

Glenys glanced at Mandy, who had stood to help the children tag their artwork so they could take their owls home after the tour. Mandy had conquered her fear by confronting the very thing she was frightened of, which is what Trista had drummed into Glenys's head. She sent up a quick prayer for guidance.

"Sure, you can give me a tour. But"—her bravado suddenly left as she thought of Heidi, the hawk, eyeing her as if she were a snack—"for now can we keep the birds in their cages? I'd rather do this slowly." She stood, and Vic joined her.

"Of course." He smiled, and she could tell it was genuine. But as they walked up the path together, he ruined it. "So, sweetheart. Wanna get married?"

❧

Tim finished with the first group of kids. He'd wondered about the actress throughout his tour. She was probably halfway to Hollywood by now.

However, as he led them back to the craft area, the subject of his thoughts came wandering down the owl path with Vic.

Well, that confirmed it. Two birds of a feather flocking together. Both could put on a good act.

He didn't know much about Vic, the new handler, but he'd seen his attitude around the women volunteers. Thankfully, none of them took him seriously.

After trading groups and leading the second up the path, he found himself distracted as he watched for Vic and the actress. The path consisted of a series of loops, and every once in a while he'd catch a glimpse of her hair, about the color of Heidi's red-brown tail.

A boy asked him a question, and he answered affirmatively, then realized he hadn't fully heard the question when one of the chaperones asked, "Are you sure? I'd never heard of owls having X-ray vision before."

"I mean, no, of course not. Sorry, I must have misunderstood."

Must pay more attention.

"Come meet Poe, our resident raven, kids." He entered the enclosure and brought out the large black bird. "Ravens aren't really raptors; they're corvids." Poe dutifully stepped onto the Astroturf-carpeted T-stand outside his enclosure. "We have other corvids here at the center, too. Magpies, crows, and jays. Ravens are the largest songbird and largest all-black bird that we know of in the world. They have been known to hunt very small prey, but mostly are scavengers."

He saw the confused looks on the audience's faces.

"Do you know what 'scavenger' means?"

They all shook their heads.

Just as he was about to define the word, Vic and the actress rounded the corner. She took one look at Poe still on his wooden stand in front of the enclosure and froze.

"I thought they would all be in cages." As she backed away, Vic looked at Tim with eyebrows raised. Tim shrugged in answer, and then Vic followed her retreating figure.

Tim shook his head. He found himself torn between wanting to help this woman enjoy God's most fascinating creations and saying *hasta la vista* and have a good life.

Once the tour was over and the kids piled onto their bus with their pinecone birds, Tim noticed a car still in the parking lot. By the sticker on the back window, he could tell it was a rental. He scanned the area, but didn't see a red-headed shrieker anywhere. However, when he entered the visitor center to go to the back office, she stood there with Mandy, laughing at Cyrano performing flips in his play area.

"So"—he wandered over to them—"did you decide to stick it out?"

"Yes, even though the predatory birds out there disturb me a little."

A little?

"But I can relate to this guy. He's an entertainer like me."

"*Awk.* Stick it out, sweetheart."

"And he has wonderful advice." Her laugh created a glow on her cheeks, a pleasant change from the anxious expression she had during their first encounter. He noticed for the second time the dimple that punctuated the true beauty under her pretty actress face. But he shook that thought off right away. It was easier to wish her gone if he wasn't attracted to her.

"Glenys is thinking of volunteering." Mandy passed him on her way to the office. "I'll get the information packet."

Well, that wasn't good news. The last thing Tim needed was an actress hanging out in his workplace. Alone with her now, he walked over to Cyrano and offered his hand. Cyrano stepped onto it and said, "Treat." Tim gave him a sunflower seed.

"I assume you're like Mandy and want to get over a fear of birds."

Glenys cast down her eyes to the newspaper in the bottom of Cyrano's playpen. "Yes, I have a phobia. I've been offered a career-changing role playing a falconer. If I can get to the point of holding a falcon comfortably, I'll get the part."

"How long do you plan to be here?"

"The audition is in six weeks. Meanwhile, I'm staying at a friend's cabin."

Six weeks?

Gloom hung over his shoulders like a sweaty gym towel. An *actress* at his center.

"Of course, if things go well, I could leave earlier."

Mandy entered the room and handed her a volunteer packet. "Take this home and read through it. It lays out all the jobs you'd be doing."

Tim cleared his throat as the words he was about to say stuck in his craw. "If you decide to fill out the volunteer application, I'll be hap. . .I'll do what I can to help." If he could step up the training, he might be able to have her out of there in half that time.

She perused the stapled stack of printed paper. "Thank you. Vic offered, too."

That bothered him. Vic would no doubt do more flirting than actual training and stall the process.

"You should take Tim up on his offer," Mandy said, unwittingly helping his cause. "He's also a falconer, the best I've ever seen."

"Then you're my man." The actress flashed a brilliant smile.

Tim wanted to do his own running and screaming. What had he done?

three

"I might be able to do this." Glenys had the volunteer information spread out before her on the dining room table while talking to Trista on the phone.

"Well, that's a change in tune."

"It looks like I don't have to handle any birds until I get comfortable." Her overcooked frozen dinner sat untouched. She pushed it away and tapped on the application with her pen. "Looks like I'll mostly be cleaning cages."

"Ew. And you're okay with that?"

"I would work in a barn full of manure if it would get me this job. I'm not afraid of hard work."

"And. . .what do we have in common?"

"Not much." Glenys chuckled. "That's probably why we complement each other. So, is it okay if I stay here in your cabin a month longer? I promise I won't trash the place."

"As if I haven't ever done that before. Ah, memories." There was a short pause while Trista apparently rewound some of those memories to watch in her head. "Sure, stay as long as you like. Just don't miss the audition."

They said their good-byes, and just as Glenys was feeling good about her career, her phone rang. It was Daddy.

"Hi, Dad, what's up?"

"Oh, just wondering where you are."

She hadn't told Dad of this latest adventure. But she was twenty-eight and could make her own decisions, even if he didn't agree with them. "I'm in Oregon."

"At the lighthouse?"

"No, Shady Pine."

Controlled silence. "And what are you doing there?"

"Researching a role."

"I thought we agreed if you hadn't made your big break by August, you would go back to school." She could picture his brows dipped in a frown. The Daddy Look.

"But this opportunity came up, and I had to jump on it." She had hoped to stall him until the audition. By then she would know whether she was going to become a real actress or not. "I'm in a really cool place, Dad. It's just a few miles from Crater Lake, and it's educational. I'm learning about birds."

"Birds? You?"

"I know. But the part involves handling a falcon, and all I need to do is get past that fear and the role is mine. Trista's father said as much."

"Tony Farentino?" Skepticism colored his tone.

"Yes. He said I'm perfect for the part. Why do you sound doubtful?"

"I don't know much about show business, but I've heard things about Tony. He has a reputation for promising young women parts in his films just to...uh...date them."

"Dad! He's my best friend's father! He even told me he thought of me as a daughter."

"Just be careful."

She wouldn't let Dad damper her excitement. "I'll be doing more acting in this movie than I ever did with the independent films and commercials. I have three whole scenes where I actually say something."

"Okay, but back to our agreement. A person's word is—"

"Law. I know, Dad. And law is what you do, and law is what my sister does and half our family. But it's not what I want to do."

She heard a heavyhearted sigh through her cell phone. "I'm just trying to guide you into a profession that will take care of you the rest of your life."

"I know, but do you really want me unhappy all my life?"

"You have an aptitude for this. I saw a glimmer during Trista's stalker trial. You found loopholes in my books her lawyer never picked up on."

"I had incentive. She's my friend, and I didn't want to see her hurt further." She flicked the hardened dry rice from her dinner with her fork. "Couldn't you support me? It will be my last chance to prove I'm an actress."

"Promise you'll consider dropping this crazy idea if you come against another wall?"

"Promise. But only if you promise not to push me into law if I decide that's not the place for me."

She actually heard him chuckle. "Your mother used to say you could negotiate the stripes off an alley cat. And that's why you'd make a great prosecuting attorney."

"Would she be proud of me, Daddy?" She wished she could remember more about her.

"She was proud of everything you did."

"Pray for me. Okay?"

"Sure."

After they hung up, Glenys decided not to be rattled by Dad's request, but rather rejoice because he promised to pray for her. Up until last year, he wasn't a believer. But thanks to her friends Paul and Meranda and a treasure of coins that included a note entreating the reader to believe, Dad gave his life to the Savior. Peace entered Glenys's soul and never left, knowing that should something happen to him, both he and Mom would be waiting for her in heaven.

She decided her meal was not fit for human consumption, so she threw it in the garbage and pulled out the pint of cookie-dough ice cream she had bought at Thrifty Foods on the Rogue. While spooning the sweet therapy food onto her tongue, she got to thinking. Why did most of the businesses in town add "on the Rogue"? Was it just in case you missed the river flowing smack through the middle?

The next day she showed up at the center wearing her mucky boots from Mercantile on the Rogue. She walked through the gate with more confidence than she'd had yesterday, but that didn't negate the small pool of hysteria that simmered in the back of her throat. One errant feather and she knew it would boil over into a scream.

First order of business would have been an orientation session, but Mandy and Vic had covered everything the day before. Today, and for the next two weeks, she would shadow a volunteer. Following that, the probationary period was to last two months. But, since she wasn't a "long-term" volunteer, Mandy told her their main goal would be to work on her fear so she would eventually be comfortable holding a falcon.

Vic offered to watch her throughout the day—*I'm sure he will!*—and if she had any questions, he'd be available. She was grateful Tim had also made that offer. Even though she felt animosity from him, she preferred that to Vic, a predatory creature in his own right. She shuddered. One must suffer for their craft, right?

The door to the visitor center squeaked when she pushed on it.

"*Awk.* Hello, sweetheart."

"Hello, Cyrano. You seen Tim or Vic?"

"Vic *smahr-mee.*" Cyrano bent his neck into a ninety-degree angle.

Someone had been talking about Vic around the bird and called him smarmy. That cracked her up.

Vic walked in and raised a dark eyebrow. "Having fun already?"

Glenys felt her cheeks redden. Had he heard Cyrano? "Just enjoying the parrot."

"Well, we should take him with us if his presence keeps

your eyes sparkling like that."

Oh brother. Any more false compliments and she'd walk straight into Heidi's cage and let her gnaw on her ears.

Mandy entered and greeted Glenys. "Do you have your application?"

"Right here." She handed it to her.

"Wonderful. The volunteer I wanted you to shadow isn't here right now."

"Is she sick with bird flu?" Glenys snickered at her own joke.

Mandy barely cracked a smile. "We've heard that one before. No, she just called and will be a little late. Dentist appointment."

"You want to hang out with me until she gets here?" Vic asked. He all but wiggled his eyebrows at her.

"*Awk.*" Cyrano had been chirping and making nonsensical sounds throughout their conversation. "Hang out." Apparently he also listened well.

Glenys had had enough of Vic's advances. "That's okay. You did enough yesterday. I'll just wait in here."

"It's no problem. I'm happy to do it."

He started to walk out and motioned for her to join him, but Tim entered, blocking their exit.

Tim brushed Glenys with a glance. "Oh, you're still here. Decided to volunteer after all?"

What kind of a greeting was that?

"Yes." She wasn't about to explain herself.

His lips pinched into a straight line, and he seemed resigned, like a man who had lost a bet. Shaggy hair fell over his forehead, and he swept it back into place. "Where are you starting?"

"The clinic," Mandy informed them. "That's where Camille will be working. Yesterday Glenys only saw the education side of the center. Today we're starting her on the rehab side."

"I'll take her over there, then." Vic's friendly attitude held undertones suggesting Tim had better keep his distance.

The two men locked glares. Finally, Tim broke away. "Fine. When you're ready to work with falcons, let me know." He stalked past them and into the administrator's office.

Glenys felt like a floppy piece of roadkill helplessly becoming the prize for the bigger bird.

⊰

Tim forgot what he wanted in the office. What was it about the actress that got under his skin? He so wanted to dislike her, but his admiration for her tenacity continued to get in the way.

She's only here for a movie role. She doesn't have a passion for the center.

Back in the visitor center room, he wandered over to his parrot's play area and offered him an almond from the bag in his pocket. "I don't know, Cyrano. I think the pretty actress is going to be trouble. And I don't like the way Vic has latched onto her. But it's not my place to say anything."

"*Awk.* My place."

"I mean, if she wants to be associated with someone who so obviously doesn't respect women, that's her business. And more power to Vic."

"Vic *smahr-mee.*" Cyrano bent his neck.

A chuckle escaped Tim's chest. "Camille said she was going to teach you that. Good for her."

Tim suddenly remembered he needed to check on the patients in the clinic, even though he had already done that earlier.

When he walked in, Camille had arrived. She'd already retrieved a tray of dead quail and was showing Glenys how she cut into them to remove the eggs. Vic stood over Glenys, hovering like a vulture, watching the process.

"We do this," Camille was saying, "so we can feed them to the corvids."

Tim watched Glenys's face. She seemed to have no problem digging into the dead bird with a knife, despite the mess of feathers, blood, and crunching bones. "How can you be frightened of the caged birds, yet not even flinch over this chore?"

Glenys jumped at the sound of his voice, but smiled as she glanced his way. "I had a minuscule part in a soap opera. Just my hands. The star refused to touch anything that resembled blood, so they brought me in to perform surgery for her. I knew about it a week ahead, so I studied up and watched the Health channel. Never have been squeamish. I would have continued being her hand double, but they killed her off in that same episode." She sighed. "Story of my life."

Vic folded his arms and leaned against the counter. "So, Tim, I thought you were busy." His tone held a challenge.

"I am." Tim bristled. "I've come to see how Ingalls is doing." He shuffled into the tiny room, way too crowded at the moment, and lifted the sheet from the falcon's three-foot square cage.

"I didn't know there were live birds in here." Glenys's eyes went wide as she backed up to the door.

Tim replaced the sheet over the cage. "Whoa." He sought and held her frightened gaze while trying to make his voice tender. "This guy can't hurt you from in there. He has a broken wing."

Compassion replaced the fear on her face. "Oh. How did it happen?"

"May I?" He started to lift the sheet again. If she was going to work at the center, she needed to at least be comfortable with the birds in cages. She nodded, so he removed the sheet. "A Good Samaritan found him under a pile of leaves in a parking lot. Probably hit by a car. We pinned his wing near the wrist joint."

She took a step closer. "What kind of bird is it?"

"A prairie falcon."

"A falcon?" She reached behind her without taking her eyes from the bird and fumbled for the door handle.

"I'm praying he heals so we can release him, but the prognosis isn't good."

"You're praying?" A small grin dawned on her face.

He liked the positive response. "I pray over all the birds here." With an involuntary dart of his gaze to Vic, who was now preoccupied in a flirty chat with Camille, he added, "And some of the people." He shrugged. "Anyway, Ingalls is on the mend—"

"Ingalls? How do you people name these birds?"

Camille joined the conversation. "I named him after Charles Ingalls, you know, *Little House on the Prairie*? Pa?"

"Oh," Glenys nodded. "Because he's a—"

"Prairie falcon," they said together.

Vic leaned against the counter and folded his arms. "Because of Camille, we've had patients named Edwards, Garvey, Harriet, and. . ." He tapped his temple, apparently trying to remember.

Camille rolled her eyes. "Half-pint. The fledgling? How could you forget her?"

"Sorry. If they'd all been named after *The Terminator* movies, I might have remembered."

Camille slapped his forearm. "Men!" She looked at Glenys while Vic rubbed his arm. "I'm afraid I have a short day today. I could only come in long enough to prepare the food. Totally forgot about a kindergarten program at my son's school."

"I'll continue her training," Vic said. "And by the way, that hurt."

"Oh, you'll live, you big baby."

"No," Tim piped in. "She needs to be exposed to falcons." He turned his head to look at her. "Right? Do you mind if I take over your training?"

A wide, genuine smile blossomed on her face and rebirthed the dimple he'd enjoyed earlier. "Not at all. I think that's a wonderful idea."

Vic's steely gaze darted from Tim to Glenys and back again. Then with a sniff, he followed Camille out the door. "Hey, sweetheart," he called to her. "You can beat on me anyti—"

"Shut up!"

Glenys turned her attention back to Tim. "Are they always like that?"

"Worse sometimes."

Tim felt less claustrophobic near Glenys with the other two gone. "Now, where were we?" *Falcons? Names? Oh yeah.* "We'll wait until Ingalls heals to see if we can retrain him to live in the wild again."

"How do you do that?"

"With our flight cage. It's a long enclosure where they can spread their wings and fly back and forth. I'm sure you'll see it during your training."

Glenys moved a step closer to the small cage where Ingalls eyed her, but remained calm. "He doesn't seem to be a bad bird."

"None of them are. And once you learn how to handle them, I hope you'll gain a new respect."

"That's why I'm here."

He searched her face for sincerity. What he found there frightened him more than a false heart. He saw intelligence, determination, and two lovely pine-green eyes staring back and causing his heart to beat faster.

I have to get her out of here—soon!

four

Before Glenys left for the day, Mandy asked her to tidy the visitor center. "You can find a broom and glass cleaner in the closet back by the administrator's office."

Glenys had surprised herself by the way she dug in and learned. On her second official day, she'd been exposed to all kinds of menial jobs, from cleaning cages to bleaching out trash cans. She agreed to work the afternoon shift, from one o'clock to five. She'd be more exposed to the falcons during that time. Mornings were reserved for corvids. Evenings, they worked primarily with nocturnal birds. However, she discovered she could encounter any type of bird in there for rehab.

She quickly finished the sweeping, listening to Cyrano babble from the perch in his play area. While wiping off finger-prints from the glass case containing ceramic bird-related knickknacks, she glanced his way. "You're pretty chatty today, aren't you?"

He tilted his head. "Pretty."

"Yes. Pretty chatty. Can you say that?"

He bobbed his head. "Pretty. . .actress."

Glenys stopped wiping. "What did you say?" She walked over to him.

Apparently excited to have an audience, Cyrano danced on his perch. "Pretty actress."

She glanced around to be sure they were alone. "Are you talking about me?" She pressed a finger to her chest. Who else could he be talking about? She was the only actress there that she knew of. He could have heard someone talk about a movie or television show, she supposed. But she preferred to think Tim had said those words.

"Has Tim been talking to you?"

"Tim."

She leaned on the Plexiglas wall of his playpen. "Between you and me, he was watching me all day, especially when Vic was around. Is there a rivalry between those two?"

Cyrano's head bobbed up and down as if he understood every word.

"You're a smart aleck aren't you?" She smiled and offered him a treat from the plastic container on a shelf near his playpen. Tim had shown her where it was and told her she was welcome to enjoy Cyrano anytime. "Who taught you how to talk?"

"Tim. . .smart aleck."

Glenys laughed. "Yes he is."

"Pretty actress. . .hang out my place."

"What?"

He cocked his head to the side. "Sweetheart."

Oh, now she understood. Vic must have been talking about her. Well, she would certainly not hang out at his place—ever.

Vic chose a wrong moment to saunter in. "Hi, Sweethe—"

"Ever!" She shoved the glass cleaner and rag into his hand and stalked out, leaving Vic with his mouth hanging open.

❧

The next day Glenys walked into the clinic just as Tim was putting an injured crow into a cage. She watched from the adjacent room where the food was prepared, her heart hammering until the door clicked shut. Although she'd been told it was safe while the handlers had a grip on a bird, her brain disassociated that knowledge whenever they were in a confined space. Outside, she thought she was getting better. She could be within a car's length. . .well, okay, a Hummer limousine's length. . .of a tethered bird.

Tim joined her as she stood near the dry-erase chore board.

"Glenys." He nodded his greeting. "How was your day yesterday?" He slipped his hands into his back pockets while they both looked at the board.

"Wonderful. Everything on this property should be squeaky clean, thanks to me." She noted her initials on the board adjacent to each chore she had completed.

He chuckled. "The newbies always get the peon jobs at first." He walked to the door and glanced outside. She thought he might leave, but then he hesitated. "Are you working with Camille today?"

"I guess. She's the one who showed me how to clean the buildings. I'm assuming we'll work outside today."

"Would you like to follow me around until she gets here?"

Warmth spread throughout her chest. "Yes, that would be nice."

He opened the door wider and invited her through. "It might not be too nice. I'm headed to the breeder barn."

"Where the mice and chicks are?" She could think of nothing better.

With a perplexed look, he led the way down a narrow path.

"We use the mice and chicks for food, obviously. It's less expensive for us to breed them ourselves. The chicks are only fed to the permanent resident birds—those one week old going to smaller birds and the two-week-olds to the larger birds. This is so the released birds don't develop a search image for half-grown chickens as appropriate food. We can't have them getting the idea that they can hunt farm chickens."

"That makes sense."

"Day-old chicks are okay for short-term food," he added as he palmed the doorknob of the shed-sized building. "But we don't go long-term with them because of the yolk sac. It's not absorbed by the chick until it's three or four days old. That would be way too much cholesterol for our health-conscious residents."

"Will there be a quiz later? So much to learn."

He laughed. "You'll get it eventually. It's all pretty basic when you think about it."

"Sure, for you."

They entered, and Tim flipped on a fluorescent shop light that flickered to life, revealing various styles of cages and containers for the living creatures inside. They lined the walls with barely enough room for two people to pass. On the right, baby chicks peered out at Glenys from behind metal screens. On the left was a system of hanging plastic drawers, about four inches deep. They were stacked seven high and ten wide. Warming lights created a tropical atmosphere, despite the cool air outside.

"What's in here?" The labels all said BREEDING FAMILY.

Tim pulled open one of the drawers. A mouse nest with three adults and a mess of thumb-sized, furless babies seemed quite comfortable on wood pellets and strips of newspaper.

"Oh, this one looks like Jack." She pointed to a dark mouse with a pink nose. "He was a pet when I was little. My best friend until. . ." A lump formed in her throat. She hadn't cried over Jack in a long time. And she refused to do so now. But the tears stung the backs of her eyes nevertheless.

Tim dipped his head and looked at her with concern. "Until?"

Glenys gently shoved the drawer back in place. "Let's just say it's because of Jack I'm here."

She turned her back on the mice. "The chicks are cute."

"Would you like to hold one?"

"Sure."

He brought one out, and she cupped her hand. Its soft feathers tickled her palm.

"Um, Glenys."

She looked at him.

"You're holding a bird."

"Oh, chickens don't count."

"They don't count?"

"Well, not baby chicks anyway. My grandparents had a farm, and I'd help my grandmother gather eggs. I loved playing with the chicks." The pleasant memory was crowded out by the terrifying one. "It was on her farm when Jack. . . disappeared."

"I'm sorry." His sincerity touched her. Suddenly she didn't mind Tim knowing her tragic secret.

"Okay, here's why I'm afraid of birds. I was playing with Jack outside while staying with my grandparents. My mother had just died, and the family had gathered to pay their respects. I wasn't supposed to have him outside his cage, but I grabbed him and left because I needed someone to talk to. There was a field behind their house with large boulders that I could climb on. I sat there for a while telling him how sad I was. I started to feel better, and I left him on the rock while I got off. Before I could reach out to pick him up, a falcon attacked and snatched him away from me." She closed her eyes, forcing the hot tears back. "I lost my mother and my pet."

"It's no wonder you're afraid of birds with that imprinted on your mind."

"I didn't even realize it until we walked in here. I later learned it was a peregrine falcon. Which, of course, is what I need to work with for the movie role." A small spark of anxiety flashed in her chest, and she swallowed to keep it at ember level.

He took the chick from her hand and put it back in the cage. "Part of your job will be to come in here and take care of these guys. But now I'm concerned."

"Why?"

"You can't get too attached. All of these"—he motioned to the mice and chicks—"are food for the raptors. It hurts me, too, when we have to take a life to feed a life, but that's what we have to do to simulate the nature cycle. Are you okay with that?"

She glanced back at the drawer that had Jack's twin in it. She would have to be mature. With a straightened spine, she declared, "I'm okay."

But she may have to rescue Jack Jr.

❧

Tim had dealt with volunteers who had problems with the live-food aspect, and he worried about Glenys now that he knew her story. But if she couldn't handle it, she would no doubt go home. Which would be a good thing. . .right?

While he showed her how they cleaned the cages and where they kept the supplies, an idea plopped itself into his head. Knowing the source of that idea, he still argued. *No, I can't do that, Lord. I can't bring this woman into my home.* But the thought refused to leave.

As they walked out, the words pushed past his teeth, loosening his tight lips. "I have an idea. You have no problem holding chicks. What if we started with smaller birds? Would you like to come over on Saturday to meet my two canaries? I could show you the basics of holding a bird, and maybe you can eventually work up to a falcon."

She seemed to think about it as she slowly nodded her head. "It might work. But only if you're sure. I don't want to intrude on your day off."

No, I'm not sure. "This weekend, about two o'clock?"

"You don't know how much I appreciate this." She sighed, as if just relieved of a huge weight.

❧

By the time Saturday came, Tim had beaten himself to a pulp. He could think of a million reasons why he shouldn't bring an actress to the house. However, since she'd been traumatized as a child and it had ruined her experience with birds, he couldn't in good conscience let her remain where she was.

He glanced around his bachelor pad he shared with Gramps to be sure it was clean. She would be there any minute.

The doorbell rang shortly, and he expected to open the door to Miss Hollywood herself. But while her clothing wasn't as casual as when she worked at the center, her outfit hardly fit the stereotype. She wore a conservative pale pink sweater with a turtleneck, blue jeans, and black flats.

When she entered, her gaze swept the small living room. "This is a cool place. And right on the river. How did you score such a prime spot?"

"It belongs to my grandfather. He bought it with Grandma after retiring from the Air Force."

"It looks so rustic on the outside. I thought I'd see chinked log walls in here."

"It's just a façade on the outside. The home was built in 1965."

"*Awk.* Hello, sweetheart."

"Cyrano?" She followed the sound inside to where Cyrano's playpen sat in the corner of the living room. She put a fist on her hip, but her eyes twinkled—beautifully. "Tim. Bird theft?"

"Cyrano belongs to me. Well, me and my grandfather. We sort of have joint custody. I take him to work because the people who visit love him, especially the kids."

After she greeted Cyrano, Tim offered to show her around. "It's cozy. A total of eighteen hundred square feet comprise the first and second floors. Upstairs are three bedrooms." Realizing who he was talking to, he chuckled in embarrassment. "I'm sure this doesn't impress you. Hollywood mansions are probably more your style."

She laughed. "Hardly. But my dad is a judge. I grew up in

an upscale neighborhood and spent summers at our light-house in Crossroads Bay here in Oregon."

"Really?" Was this woman never devoid of surprises?

"I'll tell you about it sometime." She continued to wander the living room, looking at pictures on the walls and seeming to enjoy them. "I live in an apartment right now. Burbank. Trying to make it on my own."

That impressed him. She had grown up with money, but chose to suffer for her dream. Was her passion any different than his? He decided to give her a glimpse of his life. "I moved in here after Grandma died because Gramps was lonely. Although now I hardly see him. He doesn't drive anymore, but he walks to town and hangs out with his buddies." Tim wondered how long that would last with Gramps's failing memory.

"Is that where he is now?"

He shook his head, then swept that annoying tuft of hair from his eyes. "He's out with my aunt. She had the day off, so she took him to the Dom to visit a friend of his."

"Dom?" She cocked an eyebrow as she turned from the photo of him and his grandfather salmon fishing.

"The Domiciliary. A veteran hospital. He had an appointment there yesterday and found out that his friend had been admitted."

"I'm sorry. Is your grandfather ill also?" Her brows knit with concern.

"We don't know. His short-term memory seems to be failing." Tim didn't want to talk about it. "But you didn't come here for the boring 'This Is Tim's Life' tour." He motioned to the hanging bird cage in the other corner of the living room. "Come meet your trainers, Hercules and Dragon Lady."

She stopped about three feet away and peered inside. "These two tiny puffs of feathers are named Hercules and Dragon Lady?"

"Gramps named them after aircraft—an MC-130 and a U-2. For short, I call them Herc and DL."

"I'd feel more comfortable if they were named Fred and Ginger."

"You'll do fine. They couldn't be gentler." He opened the door of the cage, and she took a step back. He'd started getting used to that, but with the canaries? Seriously? "When you go to hold a bird, always give her the option of coming to you. If she doesn't feel like it, don't force it."

"No problem." Her voice held a shaky tone.

This was going to be a long day.

DL stepped onto his finger and warbled a taunt to Herc to let him know she was Tim's favorite. At least, that's how Tim interpreted it.

"Now you try. Hold your hand sideways, keeping the four fingers together and the thumb tucked. Good. Now move it to just slightly above mine so she can step up."

With a trembling hand, Glenys held it out as Tim had shown her. "I've never been this close to a bird before."

"What about the chick in the breeder barn?"

"I told you—"

"I know, chickens don't count." What a quirky woman. "Just go slowly."

DL latched onto her finger with her tiny feet.

"Ew, the claws feel icky. Take her back."

The transfer happened too quickly for DL, and she decided to get herself out of the situation. Not unusual. He often let her out of the cage, and then she'd perch on the china cabinet in the dining room. However, when he looked back at Glenys, she stood there with her hands on her head and her gaze glued to the bird.

"What are you doing?"

"Trying not to panic."

DL didn't help matters when she decided to fly a

reconnaissance mission around the room. Glenys shrieked and began dodging her.

"It's going to poop!"

Cyrano, who had been watching the lesson with interest, started bobbing in excitement. "*Awk!* Poop! Poop!"

Tim suddenly found the whole scenario hilarious. Between fits of laughter he said, "Yes, she might, especially if you scare her. Settle down."

That didn't help, and Glenys shot out the front door—with DL right behind her.

"No! Come back here." Tim didn't care if Glenys left, but DL had never been outside. Panic seized his gut as he searched the trees for the tiny yellow bird.

When he dared a glance at Glenys, she looked near to tears. "I'm so sorry. I don't know why I did that."

"Poop?" He turned on her. "That's what you're scared of?"

In a tiny voice, she answered, "To start. Then I was afraid it would land on my head and peck my eyes out."

He pinched the bridge of his nose. "Just help me find her."

For a half hour, they searched the area. Tim swallowed his dread. Anything could happen to her. There were cats in the neighborhood, cars, predatory birds. . .he had to find her. Finally he stood still and listened.

Glenys asked, "Do you see—"

"Shh. There, do you hear it?"

Glenys stood as still as a statue. Then her face lit up. "Yes! This way."

They both ran to the back of the house where DL was enjoying a refreshing splash in the birdbath. She allowed Tim to come near and hopped right onto his finger.

"You naughty girl. Now you have quite a story to tell Herc. Just don't give him any ideas."

He walked through the back door with Glenys trailing. "I'm so sorry, Tim. When the panic comes, I can't help myself."

With DL safely tucked away with her mate, Tim turned to Glenys. He'd cooled down somewhat and tempered his words. "You do realize this is irrational fear we're talking about?"

"With a canary, yes, but not with a falcon. It really could peck my eyes out."

"If you can't get near a canary, how do you expect to hold a falcon?"

She wandered to the couch and plopped herself down, looking as dejected as an orphan denied food. "Are you giving up on me?"

He dropped into the armchair. Seriously, he should send her packing. Right now. Helping her get a movie role wasn't worth his time and effort. But helping her get past her fear, and educating her about his misunderstood raptors, was worth it.

"No. You ready to try again? Or would you rather wait a few days?"

Her gaze searched his. "Really? I would love to continue. I know if I conquer this step, the next will be easier, and then the next."

He took a deep breath. "Okay. Let's try it again with Herc."

Tim put himself between Glenys and the door, and they went through the routine again. This time she managed to keep Herc on her finger. "Now that I know what to expect, it isn't so hard."

At that moment Gramps entered with Aunt Barb.

"Libby?" He offered a dentured smile.

Tim looked from his grandfather to Glenys, then back again. "No, Gramps. This isn't Mom."

His wrinkled face drooped like a hound dog's. "Oh."

That had never happened before. Glenys looked nothing like Tim's mom. But thinking back, Tim realized two years ago was the last time Gramps had seen his daughter. She'd stood in the same place as Glenys, holding Herc, and saying good-bye.

five

Tim suddenly had Herc back as Glenys rushed to Gramps. With her hand held out, she shook his. "My name is Glenys Bernard. You must be Tim's grandfather."

Tim looked past both of them to Aunt Barb. She seemed in shock, her mouth lagging open and her eyes wide. She whispered to Tim as she sidled next to him. "I'm not sure what surprises me most. That Dad has mistaken your friend for Libby or that you were entertaining a woman."

Tim ignored her remark. She had played matchmaker too many times in the past, but he always forgave her because he knew she only wanted the best for him. But now she eyed Glenys as if sizing up a prize filly. He almost expected her to nod and say, "Good teeth."

As quickly as Gramps's confusion came, it left again and he was his old self. "Name's Walt, but you can call me Gramps. You're a pretty thing. Where did Timmy find you?"

Glenys raised an eyebrow. "Timmy? How cute."

"Yeah, yeah." Tim's face warmed. "Only family calls me that." He hunted for something to occupy himself, settling on plumping Gramps's back pillow in his chair.

"I found him, actually." Glenys walked with Gramps as he moved into the living room. "He's been kind enough to teach me how to handle birds. I'm an actress researching a role."

Gramps chuckled and lowered himself into his easy chair. "For some men, the way to their heart is through their stomach. Not Timmy. Just talk about birds, and he's your friend for life."

Tim intercepted any forthcoming embarrassing stories and

introduced Glenys to his aunt.

"Pleased to meet you." Glenys shook her hand.

"Did Tim offer you anything to drink?" Aunt Barb turned toward the kitchen. "Or eat? I made apple cinnamon muffins for these guys yesterday. There should still be some if they haven't wolfed them down."

Tim groaned. "I'm sorry. It never occurred to me." He had the social skills of a barn owl.

"I'm fine. In fact, I was just about to leave."

Gramps reached for a bowl of butterscotch hard candy. "So soon? You just got here." He offered the bowl, and Glenys took one but slipped it into her pants pocket.

"Actually, Gramps"—Tim squeezed his grandfather's shoulder—"*you* just got here." He glanced at Glenys. "But you are welcome to stay."

Gramps pointed to the sofa, leaving no room to argue. "Sit. Tell me, do you know Doris Day? She's an actress, too."

Glenys chatted with Gramps for a good half hour, munching on muffins and laughing at his war stories. He had a few since he'd been a career military man spanning his tour of duty starting with the Berlin Airlift after World War II, then Korea, and Vietnam.

When Glenys finally said her good-byes, Tim walked her to her car.

"Thanks, by the way."

"Thanks for what?"

Tim motioned with his head to the house. "For helping Gramps not feel bad about mistaking you for my mother."

She waved the thought away. "I like your grandfather. Does he ever visit the center? Will I get to know him better?"

Tim wanted to tell her to stop it. Stop being charming. Stop being cute. Stop making his heart race, which meant she'd have to stop smiling. That dimple distracted him.

"Gramps visits occasionally, but not like he did when he

had a car. Now he's dependent on others to get him around. He's not happy about it either."

Her brows furrowed. "Does he have a social life at all?"

"Oh yeah. He walks to town every morning to have coffee with a group of military veterans. My aunt calls them 'the boys'."

The dimple reappeared. "Oh good. I'd hate to think of such a friendly guy wasting away."

She searched in her purse for her keys. "Well, thank you for today. This was a big help. And again, I'm sorry about your canary."

"It turned out fine, so don't worry about it anymore. I think on Monday we'll try the same thing on the smaller raptors. Maybe our American kestrel."

"Kestrel?"

"Yes. It's a very small falcon."

"Falcon?" The excitement of the day fizzled from her eyes.

"You have to do it sometime. Just think of the kestrel as a large canary."

She pressed the key fob to unlock the door with a *blip*. "A canary who can peck my eyes out."

As she slipped into her car, he smacked the roof. "No one is going to peck your eyes out. Get that out of your head."

She grimaced.

He also winced. "Okay, that was probably a poor choice of words."

As she drove off, Tim noticed the curtain in the living room move. The two conspirators were probably spying on him, wondering why he didn't kiss her, for goodness' sake. He squeezed his eyes shut. Now he would have that image to deal with.

That evening after supper, the phone rang. The male voice on the other end greeted Tim. "Hey, this is Chic."

"Hi, Chic. What's up?" Good news, he hoped. Chic

volunteered his veterinary services and had been treating a Cooper's hawk for a broken tibia.

"She's ready to come home. I'll be at my clinic tomorrow around three o'clock if you'd like to get her."

"Sure. See you then. And thanks." He hung up and looked at Cyrano.

"*Awk.* Chic."

Tim grabbed an apple and cut off a small piece, handing it to Cyrano before he cut a piece for himself. "We like Chic, don't we, Cyrano?"

"Like Chic."

He liked someone else, too. But he hated to admit it to himself. "What about Glenys? What can I say? If she weren't an actress. . ."

"Pretty actress."

"Yes, she is. And she has pretty red hair."

"Pretty red hair."

Tim said good night to Cyrano and pulled the cover over his playpen. Then he went upstairs.

Gramps sat in his bedroom, reclining in his chair and watching television. He rarely hung out downstairs in the evening anymore. He seemed to stop doing that when Tim moved his stuff in several years ago. Gramps now only had his bedroom to remind him of Grandma. Her picture sat near his recliner, and Tim could sometimes hear Gramps talking to her, probably pretending they were watching TV together.

Tim poked his head in the door. " 'Night, Gramps. I'm going to read for a little while, then go to bed."

Gramps motioned him in, a confused look on his face.

Concerned, Tim entered the room. "You all right?"

"That wasn't Libby?"

"No, that was Glenys. She's an actress who is volunteering at the center."

"Libby's an actress, too."

"I know, but they don't look anything alike." Why was this so hard for him to grasp? Did he miss his daughter so much that his mind was playing tricks on him? Tim would call Mom tomorrow and once again try to talk her into visiting.

"I like Glenys. You two ought to get together."

And, we're back.

He patted Tim's ear. "She'd be good for you."

Tim kissed the balding head. "Don't worry about my love life."

As he walked out, Gramps called after him, "Well, somebody has to."

≥≤

The next day Tim and Gramps drove the winding tree-lined road to their church. In just a couple of weeks, the five-mile drive would pop with color. But for now the deciduous black oak and walnut blended in with the evergreen pine, spruce, and hemlock.

Tim rounded a corner and pulled into the parking lot of the white clapboard church with the steeple.

Inside, after greeting their friends, they sat in their usual seat near the front. Tim turned to talk to someone behind him, and in walked a red-headed vision. He swiveled back around, elation and dread warring in his body. *She's a Christian? What are You trying to do to me, God?*

He told himself to settle down. Just because someone walked into a church didn't automatically make them a Christian. She could be a stalker. He'd prefer that right now.

Get a grip! The bigger problem was that she was in his space, his world.

Tim sighed and turned to see if she'd found a place in the packed church. There was room on the other side of Gramps, so just before she seemed to consider an already overcrowded pew, he stood and caught her eye. Her genuine smile upon seeing him made his heart *tharump* in his chest.

He asked Gramps to scoot over, and she slid in next to Tim.

"I'm surprised to see you both here." Glenys smiled. "I pass this little church every day, so decided to give it a try."

Gramps leaned forward to see her better. "Libby?"

"No, Gramps, this is Glenys, not Mom. Remember, she visited yesterday?"

"Oh, the one we talked about last night?"

Now his memory has to be good?

Glenys raised an eyebrow. "You talked about me?"

Tim felt heat rise from his collar. "Uh, yeah. You know. The reason you came over. . .training."

"Oh." She seemed disappointed. "Well, thanks again. I hope DL wasn't too traumatized."

"You kidding? She keeps asking when she can go out again."

The music must have been uplifting. The sermon must have been deep. The time in God's house must have been refreshing. But Tim wouldn't know. A gentle wave of intoxicating perfume lapped relentlessly at his senses, numbing his brain. What was it? Some high-powered Hollywood stuff meant to keep your escort light-headed? Because if so, she'd gotten her money's worth.

Unfortunately, Gramps had noticed it, too. As they walked out of the church, he grabbed Glenys's hand and pulled it through his elbow. "You smell good."

"Gramps!" Tim stopped in his tracks, expecting his grandfather to at least look apologetic for being too bold.

However, they both ignored him as they walked into the sunshine.

"Thank you." Glenys's smile didn't indicate she was embarrassed. "It's lavender."

"I knew it!" Gramps held his index finger into the air.

"Evie wore that when we first met. She was as sweet as she smelled."

Oh great. She just kept shooting down his preconceived notions of Hollywood types. She dressed conservatively, drove an economy rental car, and smelled like his grandmother.

Gramps continued charming the actress. "We always go out to eat on Sundays. Would you like to join us?"

The first thought that jumped into Tim's mind was, *No, please, no*. But the second thought pushed that one out. *Please say yes*.

Glenys glanced over her shoulder with a question in her eyes. Tim heard the words spill out of his lips, but had no idea where they came from. "Please join us. It would mean a lot to. . .Gramps."

"Okay, but only if you let me buy. It's the least I can do for all the help you gave me yesterday."

Tim agreed, but knew either he or Gramps would grab the check before she had the chance.

six

"That thing is bigger than a canary."

"Well, if I had a male kestrel it would have been no bigger than a robin. But this is a female, so she's a little larger."

Tim stood near the carpeted T-stand perch just outside the kestrel's cage.

Glenys, about twenty feet away down the dirt path, put her hand on her hip. "Do you have anything in between this one and a canary?"

Tim slapped his forehead and palmed his face all the way to his chin. "You're not picking out cars here. If you want to hold a falcon, you have to work with the birds we have."

"Maybe I should work with your canaries a little longer."

No. Definitely no. She'd already infiltrated his world by making his grandfather fall in love with her. Yesterday when they went to lunch after church, Glenys was cute and funny. Sweet and gracious. Great to look at and smelled out of this world.

Tim was miserable.

"Let me tell you a little about Kyla. It might help." She nodded, and he continued. "She was found in a cage in someone's backyard. They had illegally kept her as a pet and neglected her. As a result she didn't imprint with her own species. She's doing great now, but we can't release her into the wild." His blood still boiled over the insensitivity some humans exhibited. Criminal.

"Poor little thing." Glenys approached and nearly leaned into the wide circle he had drawn on the dirt around them. But a fear-induced force field kept her out.

50

"Now, I'm not expecting you to hold her. Just join me in the circle."

She looked down at the line and managed to scuff it with her toe.

"Okay." He nodded, happy for even a small victory. "Making a little progress. What is it about these birds, other than the fact that one took off with your pet, that scares you? Be specific."

Glenys scrutinized Kyla on his hand.

"Their eyes. Well, maybe not this one, she actually has a sweet face."

"Okay. We're talking falcons. What about them?"

"Well, maybe it's the eyebrows."

"Falcons don't have eyebrows."

"Then why do they always look like they're frowning?"

"So, basically, it's the look on their faces."

"Yes. They look mean, like they could—"

"I know, peck your eyes out."

Glenys gave him a *well, duh* look.

"Okay, I get it." *Not really.* He sent up a quick prayer. *Lord, please help this woman get over her fear. I'm running out of ideas here.* "If I find a raptor that is cute and fluffy, do you think you could work with it?"

She narrowed her eyes. "Maybe."

"Let me think, and I'll get back to you." He knew of no such bird. They were called predators for a reason. "But now I have to feed Heidi and her neighbors."

"And I still have some cleaning to do." She glanced at her watch. "I'll be leaving in about an hour anyway." Heading down the path toward the visitor center, she turned back around to face him. "Thanks again. I really am making progress. At least I didn't scream and run to my car when you brought Kyla out." With an endearing shrug and a smile, she flashed the dimple, blinding him, and headed on her way.

She was right; there had been tiny baby steps. But would she graduate from her fear in time? Tim entered the kestrel's enclosure and set her on the tree limb. He reached into his sweatshirt pocket and drew out a dead mouse. "This is for not making her freak out. . .and thank you for not frowning."

His radio squawked just then. "Tim, you there?"

He slipped the radio off his belt. "Yeah, Mandy. What's up?"

"Just got a call from the vet. He has a fledgling barn owl. Someone found him in the woods. Looked like he might have been attacked by a cat."

"Okay, I've got a feeding to do, but as soon as I'm finished, I'll set up a spot in the clinic and go get him."

A young barn owl. Cute and fluffy. *Thanks, Lord. This could provide the breakthrough we need.*

❧

Glenys grabbed the broom and began sweeping the visitor center floor so furiously she coughed from the dust. They'd had several field trips come in that day, and the students trailed in everything but the flagstone steps leading to the craft area.

Cyrano aped her cough, then added, "Sweetheart."

She stopped and leaned against the broom handle. "Oh, Cyrano. I make myself so angry sometimes."

"Angry."

"Why can't I take the next step and just get close to a raptor? That's all we were trying to do today. Tim promised me I didn't even have to touch it, just step inside the circle. I keep giving in to my fear, so I certainly can't blame Tim."

"Blame Tim."

With the handle pressed into her cheek, she closed her eyes. *Lord, I know where this fear comes from, and it's not from You. I'm tired of it and want to be healed. And not only because of the movie role. It's been a thorn in my side for too long. Please give Tim fresh ideas, and help me to be strong. Amen.*

She opened her eyes to see Cyrano regarding her with an intelligence she'd never seen in anything nonhuman. She'd been using him as a sounding board; now she felt she could confide in him as a friend.

"Between you and me, I like Tim."

"*Awk.* Like."

"That's right. Despite the looks he gives me." She remembered her lunch with Tim and Gramps yesterday. She caught him several times rolling his eyes or looking at her as if she had two heads. "But we had fun together with Gramps. Tim even smiled once or twice."

"Like. . .Chic."

Glenys wasn't sure she'd heard Cyrano correctly. She dragged the broom across the floor, getting closer so she could listen.

"*Awk.* Like Chic. . .pretty red hair."

She pushed her fist into her hip. "Who likes the chick with the pretty red hair? And am I that chick?" Just when she was opening up about her feelings for Tim, Vic's words intruded. At least, she assumed they were Vic's. She couldn't imagine Tim calling anyone a chick.

Camille hustled into the building. "Put the broom down. You've got to come see something."

Glenys leaned the handle against a wall and hurried to catch up to Camille as she ran up the path. "Is something wrong?"

"No," Camille flung over her shoulder. "I just found out Vic is holding Mouse University with his eagle, Erland. You've got to see this."

Mouse University? She hadn't learned about that yet.

They ended their scurrying at the flight cage, which happened to be the last enclosure up the path. Glenys huffed for breath while scolding her treadmill for not doing its job.

Vic stood outside the enclosure holding a small plastic

shoe box with holes punched in the top. He swept Glenys with a steamy glance. "Hi there, Green Eyes. Ready to marry me yet?"

Camille slugged his shoulder. "Get on with it. We're not here to listen to you be full of yourself."

Vic simply laughed, then entered the enclosure. Glenys stood with Camille and a half dozen other volunteers outside the broad length of the long flight cage. Erland perched on a sturdy tree limb watching Vic intently as he opened the small box and pulled out—oh no! A black mouse. Glenys looked from the mouse to Erland and dreaded what was about to happen. She slipped behind the gathering cluster of onlookers and peeked over their shoulders at the disturbing scene.

Vic held the squirming mouse by the tail and placed it in a space boarded off by wide planks perched on their sides. Located in the middle of the flight cage, Glenys assumed the plank-sided pen was to keep the victim from scampering away.

Then Vic hurried out of the cage and joined the group, rubbing his hands together. Glenys wanted to turn and run, but decided to try to stick it out. She needed to prove to Tim she could do this.

Erland spotted his target.

"So, that eye healed up nicely." Camille spoke matter-of-factly to Vic.

"We'll soon see. He's been soaring in there the last few weeks." Vic glanced at Glenys. "He had a nasty eye infection when he was brought to us. If it didn't heal, we'd either have to keep him in captivity or euthanize him." Vic's chin jutted out. "Those weren't options for me."

Despite her near hysteria, Glenys had the presence of mind to see there was more to Vic than she'd assumed.

"There he goes." It was a whisper, but held all of the

excitement of a proud dad at a kid's baseball game.

Erland landed smack on the innocent mouse, then let out a victory screech.

"Got him!" Vic pumped the air.

Panicked squeaking emitted from the tiny, helpless rodent. Glenys fought the nausea, realizing that was the same sound Jack used when he cried to her for help.

I'm so sorry, Jack.

Sharp talons held the innocent victim to the ground. A menacing beak hovered inches above, then pecked in a lightening fast movement at the flesh.

Glenys felt the bile rise.

Must.

Get.

Out.

Now!

She turned to flee down the hill while the others were preoccupied with their celebration.

As she ran past the breeder barn, her feet slid to a stop. She had to know.

The wooden door squawked in protest. She pounced on the light switch, and the white fluorescent flickered on, almost as if blinking in surprise. Remembering exactly which drawer to go to, Glenys yanked it open.

"Oh, thank You, Lord." It hadn't been Jack Jr. who'd just met his fate. She snatched the rodent and sealed him safely inside her zippered jacket pocket.

"No one is going to make you into a meal."

As she hurried to her car before anyone could see her, she knew she'd just taken a step backward in her own rehab. How could she face another predator?

seven

Glenys stopped at Paws 'N Claws on the Rogue to pick up a small cage and food for her new pet. Then she headed straight back to the cabin knowing she was going to be in so much trouble. But she couldn't allow Jack Jr. to become a Happy Meal.

"There you go, little guy." She placed him into his new home, complete with pine shavings and food. "I promise you'll be safe."

She shook out the mouse droppings from her pocket into the trash. Good thing the mouse was used to living in a shallow drawer. That probably kept him from eating a hole through her jacket.

She heated up a bowl of soup and sat at the kitchen table with Jack Jr., then called Trista and related the whole sad tale. Her friend started laughing—uncontrollably.

"It's not funny, Trista."

"I know, and I'm sorry you had to witness the attack, but. . . mousenapping?" The giggles consumed her again.

"I really thought I could do it. I thought I could stand there as nonchalantly as the others. I ted myself, and I failed."

"Yes, well, consider it a quiz for the larger final exam. That one will cost you 100 percent of your grade, which translates to no movie role for you."

Glenys swirled the spoon in her tomato soup, bobbing the croutons until they could no longer float. "I just hate predators, feathered or standing tall on two legs. The guy I just told you about, Vic, thinks if he's in a room with a hundred women, they are lucky to be in his presence. So far he seems harmless, but he targets every woman he comes into contact with. The others just laugh it off, but what if your stalker started out the same way?" A wayward thought struck her. "What if someone starts to stalk me once I'm in the public eye?"

"Now, you listen here. You don't have to be famous to attract a stalker."

"Thanks. I feel much better now."

"What I mean is, if you sabotage your career because of this fear, it's like never driving again because you're afraid of getting into an accident. Don't you believe in that God of yours?"

Smack! Trista's words just hit her with a wet rag. "Of course I do."

"Then He must not be as strong as you keep telling me."

"Okay. Point taken. God is strong, Trista." She spoke with conviction, then trailed off with, "It's me that's failing."

"I don't mean to negate your fear. I know it's real. But if I can move on, so can you."

"You're right. And I will. I have to."

After hanging up, Glenys prayed for forgiveness. *Please don't let my lack of faith keep Trista from believing in You.*

❧

The next afternoon Tim had put in his day and entered the admin office as Vic wandered out.

Mandy, who was sitting at the desk, glared at Vic's back. He had no doubt ruffled her feathers with a sexist remark.

"You okay?" Tim asked as he flipped through the day-planner book to see what was on the agenda for the rest of the week.

"That man! If he wasn't so good with eagles, I'd toss him out on his behind."

Shaking off the encounter, she swiveled in her chair and rested her arm on the desk blotter. "So, how is Glenys's progress?"

"Slow." He continued to look at the calendar, even though

he'd already gotten the information he wanted. No readings at the schools. Not even a field trip that week. "I've only managed to get her to hold a canary."

"Hey, that's a huge step for her. It's only been a week. It took longer than that for me."

He put the day planner down, turned to half sit on the desk, and folded his arms. "We tried a kestrel yesterday, but no-go. She couldn't even get close to it."

"Well, give her time. I'm very happy you've taken on this project. I can see how she trusts you." The phone rang just then, and she answered it.

Glenys trusted him. Why, he couldn't fathom. Of all the people at the center who could have helped the actress, he had been the one she'd gravitated to. Like a cat who jumps in the person's lap most frightened of it.

A heated female voice came from the gift shop. He moved to the door and trained his ear to hone in on who it might be. Glenys?

"Vic, you are the most insufferable—"

No, that was Camille.

"Hey, beautiful. You know you fear me."

Didn't Vic hear how he sounded to women?

Camille snorted. "Fear? No. Pity? Yes."

"*Awk.*" Cyrano naturally joined in. "Fear me, beautiful."

"See? Even the bird agrees."

The screen door slammed with a *whack*. Camille must have put an exclamation point on her exit.

Tim turned his attention back to Mandy. He assumed by her half of the conversation there was an injured bird somewhere.

"Okay," she said into the receiver. "I'll send someone out right away." She hung up the phone and glanced at Tim, then proceeded to scribble the name and conversation highlights in the log she kept for rescues. "That was someone from

Cleetwood Cove at Crater Lake. Their boat captain just reported a downed falcon on Wizard Island."

"How badly is it hurt?" He thanked God for people who cared enough to report fallen birds.

"It's flailing around, probably something wrong with a wing. I told them how to approach it and to wrap it in whatever they have available. They're going to do that and get it back to the dock for their usual stop at four forty-five. Could you take a crate and meet them there?"

"I just finished the afternoon feeding." Tim consulted his watch. "Sure, I can run up there."

More voices sounded in the gift shop. "Hey, beautiful."

"Hi, Vic." Glenys's voice. "Have you seen Tim?"

Tim cringed. Proof positive that this cat sought him out.

"In the office," Vic said. "But you don't need him when I'm around."

"Thanks, I'll take my chances with Tim."

"Your loss."

Tim heard the door open and close again and assumed Vic had slithered out.

Glenys joined him and Mandy, no worse for wear after her conversation with Vic. After greeting them both, her gaze brushed his face but averted quickly. "I need to talk to you about something." She glanced at Mandy. "Privately."

"Can it wait until later? I'm about to run up to Crater Lake to get an injured bird."

"Oh." Her disappointment dragged her expression to a frown. "It can wait then."

"Would you like to come with me?" Wait. Who said that? He'd better have a stern talking to his mouth before it got him into trouble.

"I'd love to." There was that smile and the lethal dimple. "I have a fairly light workload this afternoon. I'll see if I can get away."

Mandy sealed his dumb idea. "You can go, Glenys. There's a person coming in today who is interested in volunteering, so I can have Camille show her your jobs. Then we can promote you to the clinic if you're comfortable with that."

A haunted look passed over her eyes. "But I haven't graduated to holding a bird yet."

"That's okay." Mandy leaned back in her chair. "You'll only be assisting when we're treating a patient, and the rest of the time you'll be cleaning, stocking supplies, and filing."

A tiny look of relief softened her demeanor. "Oh. . .well, I can do that."

"So, are you going with me?" Tim checked his watch. About an hour's drive up there and another half hour to hike to the boat dock. "We need to get going."

Glenys nodded, then followed him out. "I've never been to Crater Lake."

"Really? Do you have a camera?"

"In my car." Whatever had haunted her in the office had ebbed away. She now spoke with animation, as if excited to take this adventure.

"Why don't you get it and meet me out front? I have to get some equipment to take up there."

She rushed to the door, but turned before leaving. "We can talk on the way up then."

"Sure."

After she left, he slapped his forehead over just making himself a captive listener.

Mandy also passed him on her way to the door, leaving him alone with Cyrano. During a quick food and water check, knowing they wouldn't be going home soon, he said, "I'm having a hard time resisting those green eyes."

"Green eyes."

"But it's that dimple I fear most."

"Fear. . .me."

Tim shook his head. "I should put a restraining order on Vic to keep him away from you."

After loading his SUV, Tim and Glenys began the fifty-mile excursion up the mountain. He loved this drive, no matter the time of year. At this elevation the leaves were beginning to turn. Hints of gold and scarlet peeked at them through the Douglas fir as they snaked their way up the two-lane highway.

Glenys sat with her hand-sized digital camera out of the case, ready to snap away.

"So," Tim ventured. "What do you want to talk to me about?" Best to get it out of the way if it was something unpleasant, which he assumed it was by the concerned look on her face earlier.

She chewed her thumbnail. "Vic's eagle attacked a mouse yesterday."

"I heard—isn't that great? He's been working with Erland forever it seems."

"I was there. I watched it."

"Cool!" He glanced over to see her face—not excited by any stretch of the imagination. Then he remembered their conversation in the breeder barn about her pet mouse. "Not cool, huh?"

"No. I was back at my grandparents' ranch, and the little girl in me freaked out."

"But I know Vic and Camille were there. They didn't say anything about you running and screaming."

"Well, I didn't, exactly." She moved from thumb-chewing to finger-chomping, as if she were trying to hold in the words. "I left quietly. I doubt they even knew I was gone. They probably thought I'd just left out of disinterest."

"Okay, well, that sounds good. You're making progress."

"If I had just continued walking to my car, you could have called it progress."

"But. . .you stopped? What are you trying to not tell me?"

"Istoleamouse!" It all jumbled out of her mouth after, he assumed, being held behind her teeth for so long.

"What?" He whipped his head toward her just as they entered a curve. Bad move. They swerved slightly, and he had to jerk the wheel to get them back on the road.

"Jack Jr."

Now she was speaking in code. "Glenys, I don't understand."

She took a huge breath. "I stopped at the breeder barn and took the little black mouse that looked like Jack."

"Jack. . .the mouse you had as a kid that the falcon flew away with?"

She nodded her head, tears brewing.

"To save him, I'm guessing."

"Honestly, I've never done anything like that before. I never shoplifted as a kid, never took pens from businesses unless they were meant for that, never fudged on my taxes—"

"Whoa." A chuckle bounced in his chest. "You think I'm going to fault you for trying to save one of God's creatures? That's what we do at the center. You just decided to rescue the food used for the creatures we're trying to save."

"Then. . .I'm not in trouble?"

He shook his head. "Not as long as you stop at one. If I see all the mice on the lam tomorrow, I may have some concerns." He winked, hoping to relieve her anxiety.

Her shoulders straightened, as if she'd just released a huge weight from them.

"Um, Glenys, what was it you called the mouse?"

"Jack Jr."

He smiled. She was going to have an interesting surprise in a few days.

❧

Glenys glanced at the attractive man sitting next to her. At times he seemed distant, as if her very presence caused discomfort. At others, like today, he laughed with her, teased her, and, dare she say—flirted a little.

His smile came easily, and she enjoyed watching it spread to his eyes. Nice eyes. Brown with bursts of gold.

After a while they reached their destination north of the lake, the Cleetwood Cove trailhead parking area. Tim pulled in, but before opening the door said, "I forgot to tell you. The trail to the boat dock is about a mile with a steep grade. Would you like to wait here?"

She glanced down at her ugly work boots. Comfortable and durable. A far cry from the Manolo sandals she wore to a party Trista's dad threw for some Hollywood players last month. "No, I'm sure I can make it."

Before they got out, he pulled his cell phone from his shirt pocket and threw it into the glove compartment.

"What if you need that?" She pointed to the dash.

"I don't like taking it on a water rescue. I dropped it in the river once, and now I guess I'm overly cautious."

She hopped out and, slipping her camera into her jacket pocket, watched him remove the plastic crate from his vehicle.

He held out a small backpack. "Think you can carry this? I have a few bottles of water, some protein bars, and the first-aid kit in here."

She weighed it in her hand and knew she'd have no trouble carrying it. She followed him down the neatly graded trail.

He wasn't kidding. At times she felt she was trudging the inside of a large cereal bowl. Tim's average size hid the fact that he was incredibly fit. Glenys puffed like the city girl she was, and she vowed to join a gym when she returned home.

He glanced back at her, grinning. "What do you think of the lake?"

She hadn't been able to enjoy the lake up to that point, but now took in the grandeur and beauty. She stopped briefly to take a picture. "It certainly is round."

"Yep, craters usually are."

She could see glimpses of cars along the rim drive in places where it neared the edge. From there pine trees softened the harsher landscape of sheer rock walls and ancient volcanic flows. But all of that paled against the star of the show, the lake, brilliant and pure. "I've never seen such clear, blue water."

"This isn't a stream-fed lake, so no silt or mud can trail into it. What you see is melted snow and rain. There are also no outlets, so the water just seeps down into the caldera. This is the deepest lake in America, which also accounts for its color."

They continued to walk, him easily carrying the crate by the handle and her struggling for breath.

Again, he looked back at her. "You okay?"

She nodded, but couldn't speak.

He glanced at his watch. "Let's rest a moment. We'll make it down there before they dock. You can take that backpack off, and we'll have a snack."

As she removed the extra weight, cooling sweat trickled between her shoulder blades. They sat on a fallen log and dug a couple of water bottles out. She resisted the urge to chug it. "I can't imagine taking this hike in the summer. The air is cool now, but the exertion is making me warm." She took another sip and held the liquid in her mouth while letting it trickle slowly down her throat.

"In the summer the mosquitoes are relentless. This is a good time of year to hike down." Tim dug out two chocolate–peanut butter protein bars and handed her one. "I know this is the whirlwind tour. Maybe we can come back sometime so you can enjoy it."

The fact that he said "we" did not go unnoticed.

"Here's the abridged tour." He pointed to a cone-shaped

offset island. "That's Wizard Island, named by William Steel in the 1880s because it looks like a wizard's hat. It's the cone of an extinct volcano within a dormant one."

After taking a bite of the protein bar, he pointed to the far rim. "See that dark island near the wall?"

She squinted, but she could barely make out a rough, rocky, and unfriendly looking island.

"That's the Phantom Ship. If you drive the rim and look for it, it disappears and reappears as it blends into the wall depending on your location. The sun's position also contributes to its name."

"This place is amazing." Her eyes couldn't take in enough, and her brain couldn't process everything she saw.

"That's nothing. I don't have time to show you Pumice Castle, Vidae Falls, or Devil's Backbone." He put their empty water bottles and wrappers in the backpack and helped her put it back on. Then he grabbed the crate again. "Or The Pinnacles, Dutton Cliff, The Wineglass." He spread his free arm out. "It's advertised 'Like No Place Else on Earth.'"

"Okay." She laughed. "I get it. I need to come back."

He continued down the trail, and for the next fifteen minutes, she watched the back of his head. Out in the water, the small open tour boat with about seven passengers chugged back from the island, and by the time Tim and Glenys reached the dock, it was just pulling in.

Passengers filed out, talking with excitement about their unplanned passenger. They hung around, eager faces ready to see the bird guy work.

Tim set the crate down on the dock, opened it, and drew out his thick falconry gloves and a blanket. He tossed the blanket over the crate and slipped the gloves under his arm, and then he touched Glenys's shoulder. "You can wait on the dock."

She nodded, then pulled out her camera and began documenting the scene with stills. Standing at the edge of the dock looking down into the boat, she could clearly see everything.

The captain greeted Tim as he boarded. "We did what the lady at the center said." He motioned to a young man, about twenty years old, sitting in the back of the motorized skiff. He wore jeans and a white T-shirt. "This gentleman here found the bird and offered his overshirt to wrap it in." At the man's feet was blue chambray with an obvious lump in it.

Glenys felt her heart palpitate.

Tim knelt next to the bundle but looked at the man and extended his hand to introduce himself. "Tim."

"Ethan."

"Thanks for taking good care of this little guy, Ethan."

"No problem. I felt really bad. It was flopping around near the trail."

Tim cupped the blanket in his hands and spoke to Glenys. "I'm determining how he's facing. Don't want to get the beak end."

Visions of Tim losing a finger threatened to blot out rational thought. Glenys's perspiring face went cold.

Apparently satisfied, he donned the gloves and lifted the shirt just enough to peek inside. "I think we have a female peregrine here."

A peregrine! Please, God, no running and screaming in front of these people. Don't let me embarrass Tim.

After a little more inspection, he turned sad eyes to Ethan. "And she has a broken wing."

"How could that happen?" Glenys asked, trying to feel Tim's compassion.

Tim looked out at the island, then up in the air. "Oh, could have been an altercation. Maybe she was injured enough to fall and broke the wing upon landing. You never know."

He again cupped the shirt around the bird, which looked about twenty inches long. "I'm going to carry her to the dock.

Then we'll transport her to the crate."

Once he passed Glenys, he motioned with his head. "Grab the blanket, please."

She did so and tried to hand it off to him as he knelt near the crate's open door.

"No." Tim looked up at her, still grasping the bird's middle. "I need you to drape the blanket over her and the crate, and then I can work to get the shirt off. Together, we'll transfer her into the crate."

"Together?" Hysteria began to climb up her throat.

Tim's look pierced through to her heart. "What I mean is, you'll hold the blanket so it doesn't slip while I scoot her inside."

Ethan approached. "May I do it? I kinda feel like she's mine."

Glenys jumped on the request. "Sure!" Relief flooded her, but as she looked back to Tim, she saw the disappointment in his eyes. The Shady Pine Raptor Center emblem on the polo shirt under her jacket burned accusingly through to her skin. She lifted her hand to pluck at it. The men proceeded, and she continued to take pictures, squelching the guilt.

Ethan did as Tim had asked and draped the blanket over the falcon and the open crate. Tim worked to free the bird of the shirt, while the blanket kept her calm.

His gentle voice also soothed the bird. "There, we'll get you fixed up. . .no worries. . .good job. . ." Then he placed her inside onto another blanket. Ethan let the first blanket fall over the crate.

The crowd of about twenty people now clapped, but Tim shushed them. "We don't want her nervous, do we?"

They all nodded and cheered in whispers.

Back on the steep path, this time going up, Ethan and his girlfriend joined them. Glenys tried not to hate the thin blond beauty wearing a purple hoodie and tan hiking shorts for her ability to keep up with the men. Glenys's legs ached after only five minutes, so she fell behind. Still, she could hear Ethan's incessant barrage of questions about the center.

By the time she caught up to them at the midway point, they had already rested for five minutes, but Tim patiently waited for her to get her second wind.

She pointed to the crate. "Isn't that heavier now with the bird inside?"

Tim glanced down at the blanket-covered carrier. "Not too bad. She probably only weighs two pounds."

Ethan spoke up. "I can carry her the rest of the way."

"You sure?"

"I kinda feel like she's my responsibility." Ethan stood and brushed off his jeans.

That signaled the end of the break to everyone else.

Glenys could barely feel her numb toes from the earlier hike down into the caldera. Now her upper leg muscles twitched in protest for having to climb. Knowing they had to get the patient back, though, gave her new resolve, and she joined the others—slowly.

At the top, Tim waited for her, the bird already safe in the back of the SUV.

Ethan was shaking his hand. "Thanks for the business card. I'll come by to check on her and maybe see how I can volunteer."

"We can always use help."

On the way back to the center, the thick silence in the car weighed on Glenys's chest. Finally, she rallied her courage. "I'm sorry."

"For what?" Tim's eyes never wavered from the road.

"For not helping back there. I hesitated for only a second when you asked me to work the blanket, but then Ethan stepped in. I know I would have been able to do it." She fidgeted with the digital camera in her lap, rubbing at the screen with her shirt to remove the fingerprints. "I should have refused his help and done my job. But the bird is a peregrine falcon."

Peregrine. Her enemy. The bird that had become her token for loss. For her mouse, Jack, yes. But symbolically for her mother. Why couldn't she step beyond that fear?

They came to a T intersection where the highways met, and he turned left.

Glenys chewed her thumbnail. "Aren't you going to say something?"

"What do you want me to say?" His voice lay even, but a nerve jumped in his jaw.

"I don't know. Maybe forgive me for letting you down?"

Tim glanced her way briefly. "You let yourself down."

She turned her gaze out the window, where evening shadows had begun to gray the mountain road. "You're right."

Long breaks of silence were intermittently dotted with small talk for several miles. But the mood lightened, and by the time the road straightened out, they chatted comfortably once again.

Glenys turned on her camera to look at the pictures on the screen. She had snapped nearly fifty images in the short time between removing the bird from the boat and placing it in the carrier. Tim's professional determination to keep the bird safe showed clearly in the small screen, and she thought of her fear. Tim had taken authority over the falcon's fear just as God wanted to take authority over her fear. In the silence of the car, she heard a whispering in her soul. *I can do everything through him who gives me strength.*

Thank You, Lord, for sticking with me. She also thanked Him for Tim, a patient man who looked more attractive inside and out to Glenys every day.

eight

They arrived back at the center, and Glenys followed Tim as he carried the falcon to the clinic. Mandy had called him while they were on the road to say the vet would meet them there.

Glenys's shift officially over, she checked her watch as her stomach grumbled. The protein bar had worn off. "I guess I'll go home now, unless you need me for anything else."

"No, that's okay." His gaze swiveled to a different cage, one she knew had been empty yesterday. Now it had a sheet over it. "Before you go, though, come meet another patient." He lifted the sheet.

As she peered inside, two very large black eyes peered back, nestled inside a sweet heart-shaped face. "It's an owl!"

"A barn owl, to be exact."

"Have you named it yet?" Glenys could tell it was young by the downy white tufts sticking out from brown feathers, making it look like it had just lost a pillow fight.

"No. Haven't had time. He came as I was getting off yesterday; then we had the emergency today."

"He looks vaguely like my high school drama teacher, a very sweet, creative little man. We all loved him. His name was Mr. Dunkel, but we called him Dunk. Ooh!" She bounced as the idea hit her. "Can we name him Dunk?"

Tim's smile almost looked smug. "Dunk it is. Would you like to help take care of him?"

"Do I have to touch him?"

"Not until you're ready."

She looked back at Dunk, who regarded her with the

70

wisdom of his species. Plus something else. Trust.

"Yes. I think I'm ready to get closer."

Before she left the grounds, she stopped at the visitor center to retrieve her purse. She'd forgotten to take it in her excitement.

Cyrano sat on his perch. "*Awk.* Hello, sweetheart."

She opened the plastic container and gave him a pine nut. "I had a wonderful day today. I think I'm about to conquer my fear."

"Fear."

"And don't tell anyone, but after spending the day uninterrupted with Tim, I'm really seeing the beautiful side of him."

"Beautiful."

"Maybe I shouldn't say that about a guy, but I don't mean his looks, which are great, too, but he's beautiful on the inside. He was so gentle with that falcon today. It barely ruffled its feathers. Whether Tim admits it or not, he's a beautiful person."

"Beautiful. . .green eyes."

"What? Who is talking to you, Cyrano?"

"Fear me, beautiful green eyes."

Alarm shot through her spine. Different than the other sexist remarks Cyrano repeated, this one could be dangerous. Was Vic plotting something? Was he more of a stalker than the women at the center gave him credit for? She shuddered.

After pulling her purse from the desk drawer in the admin office, she drew out her key chain–sized can of mace. Then she hurried to her car in the growing darkness.

When she pulled up to the cabin, a strange car was parked in her spot. And even more curious, the lights were on inside the cabin. She sat in her car for a few minutes, trying to decide whether or not to call 911. She quickly dismissed the thought. Certainly a robber, or stalker, wouldn't leave a car in plain sight and the lights blazing. Not even Vic. . .would he?

Get a grip, and see who has invaded your space.

Before she could step onto the porch, she heard a screech inside. A happy one. One she recognized. The front door burst open, and her robed and freshly showered friend swept her into her arms. "Trista?"

"Surprise!"

"Yes, it is."

Trista hugged her and pulled her inside. "You'll never guess what I did today."

"Um, fly to Merrick, rent a car, and show up here? Unannounced?"

"Well, yes, but guess what I did between renting the car and showing up here." They plopped down on the sofa where Trista already had a glass of white wine on the coffee table. She must have seen Glenys glance at it. "You want one?"

"No, thank you. You know I don't drink." Glenys's mind spun in the gust of Trista's whirlwind.

"Anyway," Trista continued, as if her sudden appearance were as natural as a walk down the red carpet. "I stopped in at your raptor center to surprise you, but you weren't there."

"I went on a bird rescue." Those were six words she never thought she'd say. "I'm sorry I wasn't there for your surprise."

"Actually. . ." Her eyes twinkled.

What was she up to?

"The surprise wasn't me." She threw her arms wide. "It was that I decided to volunteer at the center, too."

"Excuse me? Why would Little Miss Director's Daughter don mucky boots and slave at a smelly bird center?"

Trista's arms dropped. "To support my friend, of course."

Glenys's insides went all mushy. "Were you the one Mandy said was coming to take over my duties?"

"That's me. Actually, besides supporting you, I want to learn about the place from the ground up and give a donation."

"That is so cool! When I become famous, I'll do stuff like that." Caught up in the excitement, Glenys had questions about the process. "So, is there a crew here filming your every move? Will it be documented on reality TV? Will you present them a check in a ceremony?"

Trista reached for her wine and quietly sipped during Glenys's inquisition. "Actually"—her subdued voice didn't sound like Trista at all—"I've asked the lady at the center—"

"Mandy?"

"Yes, Mandy. I've asked Mandy to keep it quiet that I'm here. I'd like this to be low-key."

"You? Low-key?"

"I know." She shrugged and ran her finger around the rim of the glass. "I'd just prefer it this way for now. Okay?"

Glenys narrowed her eyes. Trista's activities were always media magnets. She couldn't sneeze without it being reported in a gossip rag. Maybe she'd gotten tired of playing the game and just wanted some normalcy in life.

"Okay. I won't say a word."

"Thanks." Trista leaned forward and tilted her head in a conspiratorial position. "Now, what can you tell me about the tall guy I saw walking with an eagle. Dark hair, thin mustache?"

"Vic?" No! She couldn't have her sights set on Vic. She could hear Cyrano repeating, *Fear me, beautiful green eyes.*

Trista took a sip of her wine. "I was going to introduce myself, but the director suggested I should keep my distance. Does she have a thing for him or something?"

"Mandy? No. Vic is a womanizer, and she was warning you. I'm surprised you flew in under his radar."

"Me, too." Her face screwed into a miffed, I-can't-believe-someone-didn't-notice-me look. "He must have been preoccupied." She trailed her index finger around the rim of her glass. "Is he attached?"

"I just told you, he's a womanizer. You shouldn't want to have anything to do with him."

"Maybe." She dragged out the word and took another sip.

Perhaps it was a blessing that Trista decided to come. It would give Glenys the opportunity to present her Christian worldview in an up-close, personal kind of way.

Trista drained her glass and rose, no doubt to refill. From the kitchen Glenys heard a shriek. This time not in such a good way. She ran to see what happened.

Trista was pointing at the mouse cage.

Glenys frowned. "You knew about Jack Jr. Why are you freaking?"

"Because of those! What are they?"

Glenys leaned down to get a better look. Six tiny flesh-colored blobs cuddled together. "Hmm. I guess Jack Jr. is a Jacqueline."

nine

Wednesday afternoon Tim checked on his two new patients, Dunk, the barn owl, and the female peregrine falcon from Crater Lake. Chic had spent the night before working wonders with the broken wing. Now she just needed to recuperate.

"What should we call you?" He regarded the falcon. "Lady of the Lake. Yeah. Lady for short. How's that sound?"

Lady tilted her head as if trying on the name.

"Time for rest, okay? We'll have you up and out of here in no time."

As he replaced the sheet over the cage, Glenys entered the clinic with a woman in tow. By her expensive-looking gold-hoop earrings, leather jacket, and designer jeans, he wondered if she was an investor. "Tim, this is my friend, Trista Farentino. Mandy showed her around yesterday. She's going to take over my duties."

Wearing that?

"You look familiar." He searched his memory.

She tittered and struck a paparazzi pose. "Did you see my latest movie, *Love Stinks*? It was a romantic comedy."

Another actress. He shook his head. *Lord, what are You doing to me?*

She placed a manicured finger on her chin. "Hmm. You don't look like the romantic comedy type. I was also in several adventure movies, including *Danger Down Under*, the third in the spy-thriller franchise. I played Agent Risk. Did you see that one?"

"No. I don't have time to go to the movies." Two actresses. Two thorns in his side. Suddenly remembering where he saw her, he snapped his fingers. "You were on the news last night."

Her face fell. "The stalker." She nervously glanced toward Glenys.

"Wait." Glenys looked from Tim to her friend. "Last night?"

Trista turned to Glenys, looking smaller and more vulnerable than she had when she breezed in. "He's getting out today. Good behavior." She snorted a disgusted half laugh.

Glenys balled her fingers into fists. "Why didn't you tell me?"

"It's no big deal." Her gaze shifted to the ground.

"After what you went through? How are you feeling about this?"

"I have a restraining order." Trista lifted one shoulder and dropped it. "What am I supposed to feel?"

"Something. You're supposed to feel something."

Glenys followed Trista out the door. Tim didn't mean to eavesdrop, but they weren't exactly having a private conversation.

"Don't try to thrust your fear on me." Trista's voice bordered on shrill. "You're the one with a predator problem. How did my situation become yours?"

"I can't believe you're making this about me."

And these are best friends? Tim shook his head as he placed a chicken carcass in Lady's cage. She reached out and grabbed it with her sharp talons, then proceeded to rip at the feathers to get to the meat.

He'd take birds over women any day. At least they had a purpose for ripping each other apart.

After a few moments he hadn't heard anything from the two outside and assumed they'd left, but when he opened the door to attend to his other birds, both women were hugging and apologizing.

Oh brother. Two drama queens.

His radio squawked. "Tim, this is Mandy. Come to the office, please."

He left the clinic and slid past the two women still locked together.

When he reached the admin office, he pulled up short upon seeing Mandy's furrowed brow. "It's your grandfather."

"Gramps?" His heart thudded to his gut. "What happened?"

"He's missing. Your aunt just called and said she dropped in over there and he was gone."

"Thanks, I'll call her."

He slipped his cell phone from his pocket, not too worried. Gramps probably just walked to town. But why would Aunt Barb call about that?

When she answered, her voice held a borderline panicked tone. She told him what Mandy had already related.

"Did you check his favorite places? The diner? The barber?"

"I called around, but no one has seen him."

Tim's alarm rose just a little, but he knew Gramps couldn't go far. Until she told him a neighbor saw him leave at eight o'clock that morning. Tim checked his watch, although he knew it was well after noon.

Aunt Barb continued. "I know he goes to breakfast with his friends, but isn't he usually back in a couple of hours?"

"I'll look for him in town. Don't worry, he probably just lost track of time."

As he headed to his car, she added, "Cyrano's missing, too. You did say you were leaving him home today, right?"

"Yes, Gramps said he wanted to spend the day with him." He hopped into his car and slipped the key into the ignition. "Nothing unusual about Gramps taking Cyrano to town, but you're right, he never stayed away this long."

"I'm worried, Tim. What if he never made it to town? What if someone picked him up thinking he was a hitchhiker? What if he fell in the river?"

"Hey." Tim knew his aunt was about to work herself into a frenzy. "Gramps has lived here a long time. Don't worry. I'll go to town, but you can pray he stays put wherever he is so I can find him."

"Okay." The small tenuous word tugged at his heartstrings. "I'll stay here in case he comes home."

"Don't you need to get back to work?"

"I called. My boss said it was slow at the restaurant, but he could pull in another cook if need be."

After a weak good-bye, she hung up.

He geared into reverse, unintentionally spinning his tires.

"Tim, wait!" Glenys ran to the passenger side, hooking her fingers over the door where the window was rolled down. "Mandy told me you had a family emergency. What's wrong?"

"Gramps is missing."

"I'm going with you."

Before he knew it, she yanked open the door and popped herself in. "What are you waiting for? Let's go."

"Yes, ma'am." He nearly floored it, and they spun down the dirt drive to the paved street. Realizing how grateful he was for her support, he said, "Thank you for coming."

"It's the least I could do for Gramps. What do you know so far?"

He related the scant information he had. "Driving up and down the streets may not help. We can cruise once, but if we don't see him, we may have to search on foot. You up for that?"

She smiled, and the dimple reassured him. "These boots took me up a hiking trail yesterday. Surely they can walk through town."

He thought of Trista's little spiked-heel boots trudging the dirt paths at the center. They would be ruined by evening.

After driving around with no sign of Gramps, they parked at The Grill on the Rogue. Only a family with two children sat inside the small restaurant enjoying burgers and fries. So Tim and Glenys set out on foot.

Every place they made inquiries, from the south side of town at Tools on the Rogue to the north side at the Bait Shop on the Rogue, brought the same answers. No one had seen him.

Tim pointed toward the river. "He may have crossed the bridge. But there's not much over there. He usually stays on this side."

"Isn't it possible that once he's done visiting, he'll go home?" Glenys pulled her hair off her neck and clipped it with a brown plastic barrette.

Tim shook his head. "He's never been out this long before. And he always goes to the same places. This town isn't that big. Where could he be?"

They headed for the bridge, and he noticed for the first time Glenys's bare neck had a freckle. A heart-shaped freckle. He averted his eyes. Now was not the time to be thinking of heart-shaped freckles.

They continued to ask people on the street, but no one had seen him. Finally, a couple dressed in hiking gear passed them, talking to each other. "What a crazy old guy!"

Tim stopped them. "Excuse me. You've seen an elderly gentleman?"

"Yeah." The woman pointed over her shoulder. "At the RV park. He's entertaining people over there, telling funny war stories."

"And his dancing parrot is a riot." The man chuckled.

Glenys looked at Tim and smiled. "That's our man. Let's go."

Jogging to where they could cross the street to get to Travel Ease RV Park on the Rogue, they maneuvered the two lanes across just north of the bridge. The river ambled past them on their right.

The entrance led them to a crushed-asphalt walkway that wandered along the green, glasslike river, cutting a path through trimmed turf. To the left, on the far side of the paved road, trailers and recreational vehicles of all sizes were parked in neat spaces. They passed a pleasant park bench overlooking the river while scanning the area.

"Up there." Glenys pointed straight ahead. "See those people gathered?"

Tim peered up the path, wishing he'd remembered his sunglasses. Light reflected off the water as the sun began its afternoon descent from its apex, nearly blinding him. But as they drew closer, he saw about fifteen people pressed together near the river. Bursts of laughter came from the small crowd.

Tim looked at Glenys. "You think?"

She nodded.

They jostled their way through the people to find the traveling comedy troupe they had sought. Gramps sat at a picnic table while Cyrano tumbled and clowned around.

"Gramps!" Tim couldn't decide whether to hug his grand-father or berate him for not letting Aunt Barb know where he was. So he did both. "What are you doing out here? You should have called."

Gramps never acknowledged him, but past Tim's shoulder, he spotted Glenys. "Libby?"

"No, Gramps—"

Glenys cut Tim off. "Yes, Dad. It's Libby. I've come to take you home."

The look in Gramps's eyes frightened Tim. It was as if he were looking at them through a telescope from the past. He didn't even seem to recognize his own grandson.

"This is my daughter, everyone. She's an actress."

The crowd clapped, clueless.

She placed both of her hands onto his shoulders. "And now we have to get Daddy home. Thank you all for making his time here memorable."

"We should thank *him*, Miss." A man with a fisherman's vest reached out to shake Gramps's hand. "Your stories touched my heart, man. Thank you for serving and keeping my family safe."

Gramps gazed at him with tears in his eyes. "It was my privilege, son." He reached out to the table for Cyrano, who dutifully walked up his arm and perched on his shoulder. "Now, me and my old bird, we gotta go home."

He suddenly looked very worn. Tim whispered to Glenys, "Stay with him. I'll go get the car."

She nodded while sitting next him, and then she hung onto his arm as if he'd take off again.

By the time they arrived back home, Gramps was back to the present, tired but coherent. They walked into the house where he collapsed in his easy chair. Aunt Barb was beside herself, waiting on his every need. "Here, drink this water. I'm sure you're dehydrated. Did you eat at the diner? Do you need a sandwich?" She suddenly teared up and turned away, pulling a tissue from her pants pocket.

Tim followed her into the kitchen where she sobbed on his shoulder.

"I'm so sorry. I should have checked on him sooner."

"Hey." He rocked her. "Don't beat yourself up. It didn't matter when you got here. He'd already been gone the whole morning. We didn't know he was capable of doing something like this, but now we know, so we'll take precautions."

She pulled away and blew her nose. "I wish your mother were here. I could wring her neck for staying away so long."

"I know. Stand in line." Aunt Barb often blamed everything on Tim's mom, but this was hardly her fault. "Gramps has you and me, though. We're enough. We'll call his doctor tomorrow."

"You turned out to be a fine man, you know." She looked up at him. "I'm very proud of you."

He chucked her chin. "Between you and my grandparents, how could I have gone wrong?"

With a swipe at her nose with a tissue, she set her jaw. "I'm going to make the old fool eat a sandwich, whether he wants one or not."

"Atta girl." A rumbling from his stomach prompted him to say, "Maybe make several?"

She smiled at him and marched into the kitchen.

He returned to the living room where Glenys sat on the floor at Gramps's feet chatting away. "My family owns a lighthouse."

"Really?" Gramps leaned in, his veined hands gripping the arms of his chair.

"Yep. Maybe you can visit it sometime. It's down by Crossroads Bay."

"I know the one. I seen it plenty of times in the distance."

"Well, we're going to open it to tourists starting next summer. We have a friend whose great-great-grandfather built it, and she's requested we allow people in."

"Oh, that's fine, fine." He leaned his head back and closed his eyes. "I'll get down there tomorrow."

"Gramps." Tim decided to catch him before he slipped into unreality again. "Aunt Barb is making you a sandwich. I want you to eat, then go to bed. Okay?"

Elderly eyes snapped open. "Why, you little squirt. If it weren't for them dragonfly wings on your shoulder, you'd still be in diapers. I ain't takin' orders from you lest you got a signed note from the captain."

So much for reality.

Glenys raised an eyebrow at Tim and mouthed, "Dragonfly wings?"

"Chevrons." He pointed two fingers and touched his arm. "The stripes on an airman's shoulders."

She nodded and mouthed, "Oh."

Gramps seemed oblivious to their quiet conversation as his quick flash of anger ebbed. He gazed lovingly in Glenys's direction. "Wanna dance, Evie?"

"Gramps, do you think this is Gram?"

"Shh." Glenys touched her lips. "What did she call him?"

Tim shrugged and searched his memory. He was only fifteen when she died. "She called him Walt most of the time."

Aunt Barb entered the room. "No, remember? Her pet name was Wally, but she was the only one he'd let call her that."

Glenys stood and helped Gramps to his feet. "They're playing our song, Wally."

Tim watched in wonder at Glenys, who took on the roles needed to make his grandfather happy. As they swayed to an imaginary tune, he suddenly began to respect this actress.

ten

Trista proved to be a pain in the neck. How she thought she could do the menial jobs at the center when she'd never even scoured a toilet was beyond Glenys. Before the week was out, Trista had paid another volunteer to scrub the empty cages from the clinic, forgotten the laundry in the washer until it smelled, and nearly vomited when she walked in on Glenys slicing a quail for food. By Friday, Glenys didn't know how much more Trista could take.

Glenys had changed to the evening shift in order to work with the owls. Her first stop was the kitchen off the clinic where she picked up dead mice for the five owl residents. She made sure that each had the birds' names marked on them with a plastic card. Tim had told her all carcasses, whether it be a bird, fish, or mouse, were tagged early in the day for the volunteers. Then as they came in and started their rounds, they knew who had been fed throughout the day. However, extra dead food could be used at any time for training or rewarding purposes.

She joined Tim on the owl path on her way to the enclosures.

As they started to walk together, Trista stormed past them, muttering, "I won't do it. It's bad enough Glenys is keeping a litter at my place. But I will not feed those rodents in the drawers."

Glenys giggled. "This is probably her last day."

Tim's mouth was still open but broadened into a smile. "You think?"

Glenys strolled to Trista's side after she had collapsed at a picnic table in the craft area holding her head in her hands.

Glenys lowered herself to the bench. "Trouble in the breeder barn?"

"The smell. The wiggly little bodies. Baby mice are not cute, Glen."

"My baby mice are—you said so yourself."

"When they're safely enclosed in a hamster cage, yes. In a drawer, stacked on a drawer, stacked on a drawer—no." She started to whimper. "I can't do it, Glen, I just can't. I thought if you could do it, I could. But I can't. Don't make me go into that infested place again." She bounced her forehead off the redwood table.

Tim sat across from them. "You don't have to do anything you're not comfortable with."

Trista lifted her head, tiny shards of red paint clinging to her brow. "I know, but I admire Glenys for her dedication. And so does my dad." Her voice turned bitter. "We had a fight. He told me it was time to pay my own dues. Step out and get my own roles without his help. But I'm scared." She turned to Glenys. "I've never had to audition. I've never been in a cattle call. What if I can't do this on my own? I have no other skills."

So, Trista's problems went deeper than drawer-dwelling mice.

Glenys felt for her. But if hard work and dedication were good enough for everyone else in the business, why should Trista be any different? "Wasn't it you who told me we all have to make sacrifices in this business? Was that the royal *we*? Translation, anyone who isn't you."

"You're making me eat my words? At a time like this?" Trista rose to leave.

"Wait. I meant that as encouragement." Although, it hadn't come off as encouragement when Trista said it to her the other day. "I'm sorry. We'll figure this out together."

Trista's gaze drifted to someone heading up the path to the eagles.

Vic.

Trista swiped her face to remove the last shed tear, leaving behind black streaks from her eyeliner that made her look like a distraught raccoon. "I'll figure it out with Vic." She shot a glare over her shoulder at Glenys. "He gets me." Then she stormed up the path to follow her target.

Glenys sighed. "I don't know who to feel sorry for most. That pair is truly two-of-a-kind." She didn't think Vic was right for Trista, but at least the women at the center seemed to have a reprieve from the chauvinistic remarks. She plopped back down at the picnic table across from Tim. "Did I handle that as badly as I think I did?"

He shrugged one shoulder and stood. "I don't know. I don't *get* her." He laughed and offered his hand. "Come on. Let's feed Dunk."

They wandered hand in hand to the clinic, and it surprised her when he didn't let go. She enjoyed his gentle fingers wrapped protectively around her own. Calluses spoke of long hours building enclosures.

What dedication. What a love he poured into these creatures. If only she could pour that much enthusiasm into her love, which used to be acting. But now she wasn't so sure. Could it be possible to have two passions?

She'd made a lot of progress after working with Dunk. That little owl stole her heart the minute he peered at her through the cage. And today, before the Trista meltdown, she and Tim had visited the other owls in the nature portion of the center. He gave her his spiel about them, teaching her their habits and showing her the pellets they regurgitated from the fur and bones their bodies couldn't process. They were fascinating animals, and Glenys couldn't wait to learn more about them.

That night, after doing all the jobs that her friend had left undone, Glenys headed home. She and Trista usually drove together, but the two worked different shifts now so they arrived home separately. Glenys assumed that Trista had caught up to Vic earlier that day and coerced him to take her out somewhere since she wasn't home.

Glenys fed Jackie and all the little Jack Juniors, then showered and went to bed. Her body ached from pulling double duty. No more of that. Trista would either have to buck up and do the job or quit.

She fell asleep moments after her head hit the pillow and dreamed of Tim, of dancing with him as she had Gramps, of his hand in hers. And just as he lowered his mouth to her lips. . .she jerked awake.

"Grrr!" She slammed her head back to the pillow, trying to re-create the dream. But it was no use. Whatever had awakened her had done a good job.

She sat up. The sun peered around the blinds in her bedroom, and the clock indicated she had slept in a little. It was Saturday, and after yesterday she afforded herself that luxury. But something was different in the house.

It was quiet.

Ever since her friend had joined her, quiet nights had become noisier than a construction site. Trista snored like a jackhammer. Glenys threw off the quilt and ran to Trista's room.

She searched the darkness of the room, the shades pulled down tight to keep the rays out. No Trista. Glenys couldn't tell if her bed had been slept in because she hadn't made it since she'd arrived. Had she even come home last night?

Probably not.

Glenys checked her cell phone for messages.

Nothing.

Why wouldn't she have called if she wasn't coming home?

A horrible thought struck Glenys. Had the stalker found her? Had he kidnapped her?

She punched Trista's phone number and waited for her to answer. All she got was the cheery, "Lucky you! You got my number. Unlucky you! I'm not here. Leave a message."

"Hey, Tris? Where are you, girl? Call me, 'kay?"

She sank into a kitchen chair. *Lord, please let her be all right. As much as I hate to think it, I pray she was with Vic all night and that this stalker hasn't found her.* But was Vic that much better? Again, she heard Cyrano's voice, *"Fear me, beautiful green eyes."*

Her brain started to whir. What time did Vic work at the center on Saturdays? Wasn't it morning? She quickly dressed and drove to the center. If he was there, she wanted to see his face if he tried to lie about Trista.

When she arrived, she ran to the admin office. "Mandy," she puffed. "Is Vic here?"

Tim walked in. "Hey, it's your day off."

"Yours, too."

"Tim lives here." Mandy shrugged. "I guess we all do."

"I'm looking for Vic."

"He called in sick," Mandy informed her.

Tim grasped Glenys's shoulder. "What's wrong? You look upset."

"Trista never came home last night."

He dropped his hand. "Well, she did leave with Vic who called in"—he made quote marks—"sick."

"That's your answer? Do you just assume Trista sleeps around?"

"Hey, I'm sorry." He held his palms up in surrender. "That was out of line."

She leaned on the desk, aching for some kind of support. "Actually, you're right. It's very possible she spent the night with him."

"Did you try calling her?"

"Yes, but her voice mail picked up."

Tim nodded toward Mandy.

She picked up the hint. "I'll call his house." After punching the numbers on the desk phone and waiting a moment, she said, "Hi, Vic, I know I just talked to you, but would Trista be there by any chance?" She looked at Glenys and nodded.

Glenys held out her hand. "I want to talk to her."

"Vic? Can you put her on the phone? Thanks." She handed the receiver to Glenys, and then she and Tim left the office, giving her privacy.

Glenys pressed the handset to her ear. "Trista, what are you doing?"

After a slight pause, Trista answered, "You're not my mother. I'm not accountable to you."

Glenys heard her whisper to Vic, "I thought this was Mandy on the phone."

"A little common courtesy is all I ask." Glenys drummed the desk with agitated fingers. "Two seconds, and you could have let me know you were okay."

"And after those two seconds, you would have railed on me for doing something so stupid. You'd never have believed the truth. Right?"

Glenys gripped the phone so tight, her knuckles hurt. "When I woke up this morning and saw you hadn't come home, I thought the stalker had gotten you." She tried to hold in her sob, but it was all too much.

After a brief silence, Trista spoke softly. "Oh, Glen, I'm sorry. I didn't even think of that."

Glenys swiped away hot tears. "That's just it. You never think. What will it take for you to see that your actions affect others, including yourself?" She stopped for a moment, then backpedaled. "Wait a minute. You said I'd never believe the truth. What truth?"

"Vic really is sick. I followed him home and made him soup."

"*You* made soup?"

"I opened a can, okay? The point is, nothing happened here last night. He spent most of it in the bathroom, and I slept on his couch." She sighed. "I'm sorry I didn't call you. But I knew you wouldn't believe me. And I just couldn't take another upset."

"Yesterday was pretty emotional for you, huh?" Conviction hit Glenys in the heart.

"The whole week has been emotional. My favorite work boots are ruined. . . ."

"Those were work boots? Weren't they Prada?"

Trista clicked her tongue. "Last year's." She continued spilling her totally awful week. "I'll never get that mouse smell out of my nose. The breeder barn stinks, Glen. Then I got yelled at for leaving the inside door unlocked at a hawk cage. Really, isn't that overkill? Two doors?"

Vic hacked in the background and said something Glenys couldn't make out.

Trista spoke back. "I don't care if it's for safety. It's hard to remember both doors." She continued her tirade with Glenys. "And. . .I broke a nail."

"I'm sorry you've had an awful week, but it does get better—"

"No. I'm not cut out for the center." More background conversation, and then she came back on. "Vic just reminded me of something he suggested that maybe you and I could do together."

"I can only imagine."

"Stop it, Glen. He's not really the kind of person everyone thinks he is. He suggested we help with the reading program at schools. We could act out the dramatic parts. It could be fun."

Glenys had to process that. It did sound like a wonderful idea. Even if Vic had thought of it.

"Okay," she finally spoke. "I'll talk to Mandy."

"Great. Oh, I gotta go. Vic is shivering on the couch and needs a blanket. I love you."

"Love you, too, Tris." Even though she drove her nuts.

Glenys found Tim at the clinic, feeding Lady. She still wasn't comfortable with the bird, but managed to stand in the doorway, keeping her escape route in sight.

Tim glanced her way. "Everything okay?" He raised an eyebrow as he shut the cage door.

"Yes. She's playing nursemaid."

"Sounds like a noble thing to do."

"Mmm." She couldn't commit to thinking of Trista as noble. "So. . ." She needed to quickly change the subject in order to mull over the new development. "You're not usually here on Saturdays, are you?"

"Sometimes I pop in to help. Today I wanted to check on Lady." He peered in the cage and spoke soft words to the peregrine.

"How's she doing?"

"I don't know." Tim frowned. "After four days she should be eating better than she is. Might be an infection. The vet will see her Monday." He closed the cage and spoke quietly to the bird, then replaced the sheet over the cage

"I should call you the falcon whisperer. I've never seen her nervous around you."

"Well, we have an understanding. I work hard at not making her nervous, and she doesn't—"

"Gouge your eyes out."

"Exactly." He shoved three dead chicks into his sweatshirt pocket. "While I'm here, I thought I'd help with the feeding. Join me?"

While walking up the path to Heidi and the other birds, Glenys laughed. "Do you ever forget you have those things in your pocket?"

He chuckled. "Once in a while. A few months ago, I had

gone to feed a bird, but there was still enough food leftover in her cage. So I pocketed the carcass thinking I'd put it back in the kitchen before I left, but forgot. Went to the grocery store afterward, pulled the dead, furry mouse out of my pocket looking for my keys, and freaked out the clerk."

"I can imagine."

They strolled a little farther, and as they stopped at Heidi's enclosure, Glenys approached the subject she'd been milling about in her head since speaking to Trista.

"Vic told Trista that she and I might be able to help with the educational program. A reading thing you do at schools?"

"Vic suggested that?" He tilted his head. "Not a bad idea."

"And by the way, he wasn't lying about being sick. She slept on his couch last night while taking care of him. I believe her."

He pulled on his gloves and attached the jesses. "I'm glad you cleared that up. Sounds like Trista is blessed to have a friend like you to keep her accountable."

"It makes for some interesting arguments, though."

"Sounds like she's growing. Is it in her character to take care of the sick?"

Glenys cocked her head back and let the laugh tumble out. "No. Not even for a man." But then she sobered. "Do you think she really does have feelings for him?"

"I don't know." He unlocked the interior door and entered the enclosure. "Vic doesn't seem to be himself either. Could be because he wasn't feeling well, but yesterday he was very quiet, and I never once saw him flirt."

"Not once?"

"Not even with Camille."

"Wow. That does sound serious." He hadn't flirted with her either, but she'd been avoiding him as much as possible, especially after the "fear me" remark.

"Tim, do you think he might be capable of hurting a woman?"

He held his hand up, and Heidi stepped onto it. "Her

heart? Oh yeah. Physically? No. I think he's just a jerk."

"How can you be so sure?"

Tim brought Heidi out of the enclosure and offered her the dead bird. She didn't take it. "Because I've seen him with the eagles, the injured ones. You think I'm gentle. You should see him with a fallen bird and how he nurses it back to health. He may be arrogant, but he'd never hurt anyone. Is that what you're worried about?" He looked into her eyes. "Trista is safe with him."

She relaxed. "Thanks. Coming from you, knowing how you feel about him, that means a lot."

"And do you realize something else?"

"What?"

"You are two feet from a hawk right now."

eleven

Tim watched Glenys's face as she realized she'd made more progress. It was like a light had suddenly flicked on and shone in her happy eyes. He looked down at her feet. They never shuffled away, but stayed firm.

"Dare I ask if you'd like to try holding her?"

"No, not yet." Then the feet retreated.

"That's fine. You should be pleased with yourself."

"I am. No more screaming and running. Unless, of course, she got loose."

"That's a given." He cooed to Heidi as he returned her to the enclosure. She stepped back onto her tree limb and then snatched the food from his hand.

"I've been thinking." He locked both doors and started walking toward the next enclosure. "You've been working so hard here. Would you like a break? Heidi has a benefactor who gave me two tickets to see a play tomorrow at the Shakespeare theater. We could leave after church."

Please say yes. He marveled that he'd even asked her in the first place. A short time ago he was ready to rush her training to get her out of there faster. Now he dreaded the day she would leave.

"A benefactor?"

"Yes. Remember that first day of orientation? Mandy told you about the people who adopt birds and send money for their stay here."

"Oh, that's right. I'd love to go."

The next day Aunt Barb offered to take Gramps out to lunch after church so Tim and Glenys could make the matinee.

He thought Gramps would be upset, but as he said good-bye, the sly old dog whispered in his ear, "It's about time you dated something without feathers."

As they drove away toward Oakley, Glenys asked, "Did you and your aunt come up with a solution for Gramps?"

"She's offered to stay with him while I'm at the center. She can jostle her schedule pretty easily." He reached over to turn down the radio, a habit of his whether he had a bird or a human passenger. "Gramps has a doctor appointment tomorrow. I'm thinking it's dementia. The other day at the campground, he wasn't just telling old stories, he was reliving them."

"I'm so sorry. I know you hate to see him age."

"Gramps and Gram were the only parents I knew." He hadn't meant for that to slip, but now that it was out, he decided he might as well open up to her. "My mother found herself pregnant shortly after she graduated high school. My grandparents insisted she go to college, so they agreed to babysit. I guess they hoped she would grow up, but she was never cut out to have a kid. I was. . .inconvenient. Instead of trying to make it work as a single mom, she left me with my grandparents after college and pursued her acting career."

"I'm so sorry. How old were you when she left?"

"Five. Old enough to know I had a mother one day, and the next I didn't." He paused, reliving every time she'd promised to come home. Sometimes she'd make it, but most of the time, she'd come up with an excuse. "You see Gramps as a silly old man—" Glenys started to protest, but he waved her off. "No, face it. He does silly things in his old age, but if you could have seen the man he was. . ." His heart swelled with love. "I'm sure it killed him to see his daughter, his baby, be so irresponsible. He never spoke angrily about her, always held out hope. Still does. I think that's why he wants you to be her so badly."

"I had no idea. Is she still around?"

He grunted a mirthless chuckle. "She's in Hollywood. Been trying to become an actress for thirty years."

She stirred next to him, her gaze darting out the window.

He glanced her way. "I'm sorry. I know you've been struggling, too. But you didn't have a kid at home that needed your love."

"No. And if I had, I'd have included him in all my successes and failures. There is no way I could leave a child with my father, even though he'd make a great substitute."

"Thanks. I think I needed to hear that from your own lips, you being of the same profession and all." He turned onto the interstate. "She's still irresponsible. My aunt and I have been trying to get her to come see us for a couple of years. And now that Gramps is going downhill fast, we think she'd better come soon before he forgets who she is."

"What's her name? I might know her."

"She goes by Liberty Elise."

"Is that what Libby stands for? Liberty?"

"No, her name is Elizabeth, so she took two variations of the name and came up with the conglomeration." He remembered hearing that name for the first time as a young kid and knowing it completed the severed relationship between her and the family. "She doesn't even acknowledge that she's a Vogel."

Glenys smiled, and he almost forgot what they were talking about when he saw the dimple.

"What? Why are you smiling?"

"Don't get me wrong. You have a lovely name—for a bird handler. But on an actress it doesn't roll off the tongue."

"I suppose not. Heard of her?"

"No, but I'll keep my ears open."

"Then you're still going back."

She jerked her head to look at him. "Of course. It's what I do."

"I know. I didn't mean anything by that." Actually he meant a lot by that. His brain was telling him that she would go back to her world and no doubt forget about him and the raptor center. But his heart insisted that she might stay. Gramps loved her. Tim. . .intensely liked her. Right now he couldn't bear the thought of her leaving. So he pushed it to the back of his mind. He would enjoy being with her right here, now.

The drive into the artsy town of Oakley always amused him. Various generations of hippies wandered the tree-lined streets: the young women wearing dresses with jeans, the older with braided leather bands or scarves around their heads. Multiple piercings for both sexes seemed the fashion.

They parked and entered the large theater, quickly finding their seats—good ones, three rows back in the middle. Tim would have to write a thank-you note to Heidi's benefactor for his generosity. Throughout the play, a modern romantic comedy of errors, Tim had trouble focusing. Glenys's perfume danced around his senses, making him wish they were alone. The blue dress she wore, while not Hollywood chic, still hugged her body in all the right places, yet had been discreet enough for church.

Then there was the dimple. Even in the darkened theater, he could see it all cute and kissable.

The play finally ended, and he hoped Glenys wouldn't question him about it. He'd have to admit that his favorite part was sitting in a lavender swirl next to a kissable dimple.

They left the theater, and the crisp late-afternoon air cooled his cheeks.

Glenys checked her watch. "We have a little daylight left. Before dinner, would you like to see an alpaca ranch?"

"Whoa. That's not something I had expected you to say. You know someone with an alpaca ranch?"

"Actually, I know someone who knows someone. That's

how it's done in my circle, you know." Her eyes twinkled in their teasing.

He nodded. "Lead the way."

As he drove while she read the directions, she fessed up. "I have a good friend whose aunt owns this alpaca ranch. Apparently, Paul moved there when his uncle fell ill and ended up in a wheelchair. He became the office manager. Now he lives on the coast."

Tim cast a side-glance toward her. "How good a friend?"

She laughed. "He married my other good friend at the lighthouse my family owns."

"Oh, I like that kind of friend."

Her cheeks turned an attractive shade of pink, and she glanced down at her hands clutching the handwritten directions.

"Oh!" She thrust her finger at a side street. "Turn here."

He cranked the wheel hard. "A little more warning next time."

"No need. We're here."

They pulled into the drive, past a sign that read SINGING MOUNTAIN RANCH. A woman in her late sixties came out onto the front porch. She slowly made her way down the steps, clutching a knitted wrap around her shoulders.

She approached the car as they got out. "Are you Glenys?"

"Are you Hannie?" The woman nodded. "Then Paul says hello and to give you this." She leaned in and pecked the woman on the cheek.

She motioned for them to follow her around the back of the large house. "I apologize for moving slow. I was ill a couple of years ago and have never really bounced back."

"Paul told me you'd been in a coma. How awful."

"Not so awful. It brought my son and me together. I hadn't seen him since he was seven."

This got Tim's attention. Was she like his mother? "If you

don't mind me asking, why not?"

She pierced him with her blue gaze that cut like a laser beam. "I don't mind. It's part of my testimony. But keep in mind, young man, that people have their faults. Only Jesus is perfect."

"Yes, ma'am." He must have put too much venom into his question.

She told them about her drug use, how she forgot her child in the park, left him in the foster system. "I'm not proud of what I did, but my disobedience eventually led me to Christ. He put the pieces back together, and the final puzzle piece fell into place when I got sick. Skye, my son, responded to my plea and through God's mercy forgave me."

"That is a strong testimony. Thank you for sharing that with us." Tim found himself, for the first time, praying for that kind of forgiveness in his own family. He cringed inwardly as God reminded him that it would have to start with him. He wasn't quite ready to forgive his mother.

The tour moved to the barn out back. Alpacas of various hues grazed in the pasture, and several were in pens near the barn. A large man with a faded red ponytail came out to greet them. Hannie's face broke into a wide grin. "Meet my new husband, Tom."

Glenys's hand disappeared between the man's paws. Ironically, so did Tim's.

"Paul told me about you two," Glenys said as the couple led them to a paddock where a white alpaca eyed them with intelligent curiosity.

Hannie linked her arm through Tom's elbow. "We've known each other forever. After my husband died, Tom became my anchor. But neither of us admitted to ourselves that we were falling in love."

Tom gazed down lovingly at his wife. "It took almost losing this woman forever to know that I couldn't keep my feelings to myself."

Glenys sighed. "How romantic."

Tim contemplated that statement. He was on the brink of losing Glenys, not to illness but to something even more diseased. Hollywood. If he didn't declare his feelings soon, she could walk out of his life.

He dared to take her hand in the guise of helping her walk the graveled path in her heels, but reveled in the fact that she didn't pull away when the ground was more stable.

Evening swallowed their short time at the ranch, and after the tour Tim and Glenys ate a steak dinner in Oakley, then headed back home. Tim continued to process what Hannie had told him about forgiveness. He would have shared that with Glenys, but she chatted nonstop about the play and about the alpacas.

By the time they pulled up to the cabin, night had fallen. Glenys looked as lovely in the moonlight as she had during the day. She wore a silver jacket over her blue dress, which made the whole outfit resemble a sparkling star. He walked her to the door where she lingered while looking for her keys in the small purse she carried.

"Thank you so much for this day. I didn't realize how much I needed to get away and relax," Glenys said.

"Thanks for accepting. When I received those tickets, I thought what better person to invite than an actress?" He paused for a second, wondering why it was taking her so long to find her keys. Surely there couldn't be much in that purse. "Oh, and thank you for the alpaca tour. I'd never seen one up close like that."

"It was a great day all the way around then." She slowly pulled out her keys, but held them instead of using them.

"Yes it was."

Small talk. All meant to stall the inevitable—the first kiss. They continued to chat aimlessly while he reminded himself, once again, that she would eventually leave.

Keys jangled in her hand, as if she were alerting him to the fact that she was about to use them. "Thanks again."

Lavender perfume grabbed his head and threatened to draw him near. "You're welcome. . .again."

A nanosecond before he succumbed to the urge to kiss her, another scent cut its way through the lavender. He jerked away and sniffed.

She frowned. "What's wrong?"

"I smell smoke."

twelve

"Is it the cabin?" Glenys drew in a breath while searching the roof with her gaze.

"No, it's out there somewhere." Tim tried to look past the trees, but the darkness prevented the ability to see smoke. The smell was faint, but stronger than a nearby campfire. Tim reluctantly walked away from Glenys. "Sorry. I have to go."

"Where?" Her expression filled with concern as she followed him to his car.

"The center. I need to listen to the emergency scanner."

"Please wait just a moment." She ran back to the house, unlocked the door, and came out a few seconds later with her boots on and pulling her work jacket over the blue dress. "I can't help in high heels, now can I?"

Before he could protest, she flung herself back into his car. He opened his door and sat, but couldn't stop staring at this conundrum of a woman.

Finally, she pointed at the steering wheel. "Drive!"

By the time they arrived at the center, the smoke had thickened. Tim threw the gear in park. "It must be near."

"What can I do?" She hopped out and raced after him as he headed for the visitor center and the admin office.

Once in the office, he dug in a drawer. "Here's a list of volunteers. Call them and put them on standby. Let them know there's a fire nearby and we may need their assistance."

While she sat at the desk and started pushing phone buttons, he turned on the scanner. Sure enough, fire crews had been called in. His heart pounded as he listened intently for the coordinates. Once he heard them, he wrote them down and looked at the large map taped to the wall. "It's only five miles to the northeast, but traveling straight south."

Glenys turned in her seat, still clutching the handset. "Then it could miss us, right?"

"Unless it turns. Either way, the smoke will only get worse." He rubbed the tension from his neck. How could a beautiful day go so wrong? "Call everyone back and bring them in. Ask them to bring pet carriers if they have them. I'll go gather what I can." He started to dart out the door, but turned. "And thanks."

By the time he'd pulled what empty crates he could from the clinic, Mandy arrived. Soon afterward Camille and three other volunteers showed up, all bearing pet carriers. They stood in the darkness awaiting orders.

"I didn't smell smoke at my house until Glenys called." Mandy spoke while adding two more cages to the growing collection. "I walked outside and caught a faint odor, but I would have thought it was a campfire. Were you outside when you caught the first whiff?"

"Um. . .yeah." He didn't want to admit that he was standing outside Glenys's door trying not to kiss her. He needed to change the subject, quick. "How many handlers have shown up?"

"You, me, and Camille."

"That's it? Where's Vic?"

"Still sick, I guess."

Tim glanced around at those assembled, which now included Glenys.

"I have an update on the fire," she said. "It's turning our way."

"Okay." Mandy took charge. "Everyone, grab a carrier. If you've never handled a bird, go with a handler and assist."

Tim stepped forward. "May I say a quick prayer?"

Mandy nodded.

"Lord of all living creatures, please have mercy on this little center. Move the fire away, but I also ask that no one else is in its path. Squelch the fire in the name of Jesus. And lift up our fellow handler, Vic. Heal him, and please don't let the smoke interfere with his recovery. Amen."

Amens echoed around the small circle, and then everyone dispersed to the four corners of the center. Glenys and another volunteer followed Tim.

"I can't have you squeamish, Glenys. You have to do what I say," he shot over his shoulder as they booked it up the path to the falcons.

"I can. . .handle it."

He couldn't see her face in the dark and the growing smoke, but could tell from the tiny response that she was frightened.

They made it to Heidi, who had retreated to the farthest corner of her enclosure to get out of the smoke. "It's okay, girl. We're here." He pulled on his glove. It took some coercing to get her on his hand. He managed to get her into the carrier, though, with minimal ruffling of feathers.

"Glenys, run her down and come back for the next one."

Glenys still stood outside the enclosure. Tears streamed down her face, mumbling part of a scripture verse over and over. "God did not give us a spirit of timidity."

"I'll do it," a female volunteer said.

"Wait." He held her off against his better judgment to hurry things along. "Glenys, you said you could handle it." He hated to bark at her, but she refused to move.

"I can, just give me a moment."

"We don't have a moment." He pulled out his radio. "Mandy."

The radio cracked. "Go ahead, Tim."

"I'm sending Glenys back down. She needs a different job." He glared at Glenys, whose shoulders slumped.

"I'm sorry, Tim."

"Yeah. So am I." He nodded to the volunteer who grabbed

the carrier and followed Glenys down the path. Then he grabbed two of the four carriers they had brought with them.

He got to the next bird, still fuming. It was his own fault, really. He should have insisted Glenys find something nonthreatening to do. Over at the eagle cage, he saw Vic and Trista. She performed the same task as he'd asked of Glenys, and though she squealed while taking the cage down the hill, at least she did it.

He called over to Vic. "I thought you were sick."

"I am." Vic could hardly be heard for his borderline laryngitis. "But these guys will be dead. Which is more important?"

Well, he'd never doubted Vic's loyalty to his eagles. Just to women.

As Tim was closing the door on the peregrine, a man in his fifties ran up the hill, a blue handkerchief pressed to his mouth. He introduced himself as Chris Jenkins, and Tim recognized him as Heidi's financial supporter. "Hey, thanks for the tickets. And thanks for doing this. It goes beyond what we expect from a supporter."

"My pleasure. There's several of us here. We got a phone call about forty-five minutes ago."

As Chris hustled the cage down the hill, several other people swarmed the grounds. Tim ran to another enclosure to load another bird, shaking his head. The only list he'd given Glenys was of the volunteers. She must have seen the supporters list and called them, too. She may freeze around the birds, but her level-headed thinking may have just saved some lives.

❧

Glenys felt her fingernails prick her palms as she clenched her fists. Why couldn't she get past her fear? She'd let Tim and the center down. Forget about the stupid movie role. She needed to overcome her phobia right now, before her actions hurt others.

She noticed only one person working the owl path, Mandy. Without thinking, she grabbed a carrier and bolted to join her.

"Why are you alone down here?"

"I sent everyone to where the smoke was thickest. This is more protected, but we still have to get these guys out."

"Give me a glove."

Mandy jerked her head. "You sure?"

"I've handled Dunk in the clinic. He's only a little barn owl, but it can't be much different."

"Okay. You know what to do, right?"

Glenys nodded and entered the screech owl's enclosure. Without the heart-shaped face, this owl looked more sinister, but she kept telling herself it was Dunk's cousin. She took a huge breath, then hacked a little as the growing smoke filled her lungs. "Come on, big boy." She held her gloved hand out, and the owl stepped on. A rush of adrenaline flowed through her. She could do this. . .as long as he didn't try to fly. *Please, Lord. Keep his wings still.* She transferred him safely with only a small amount of flapping, and that, she knew, was more for balance than flight.

As she carried the cage out, Mandy congratulated her. "That's an important step you just took."

"Owls are less threatening, I guess. I know they can hurt me, but they don't scare me like the peregrines."

She nearly entered another cage when she stopped abruptly. "Um. . .Mandy? Can you get this one?"

"Can't handle the great horned owl, eh?" Mandy moved past her, chuckling.

"I think I'll work up to owls on steroids." She stayed to help Mandy with the cage, but then moved to another enclosure with a smaller, more manageable owl.

Glenys carted two of the owls back to the visitor center where she saw that the clinic patients were waiting near Tim's SUV. She loaded Dunk and another owl into the car and noted there was room for two more passengers. She spotted Heidi's cage on the ground next to Lady. She glanced around as the last remaining volunteers hustled to get out of there. She hadn't seen Tim for a while and wasn't sure she could face him.

As she stood by the cages, she chewed her thumbnail. Finally, after a quick prayer, she grabbed the hawk's cage. "Be nice to me, Heidi. I'm too big to be a snack." With her heart in her throat, and her fingers away from any holes, she slid it into the SUV. Coming back with all digits and eyeballs intact, she decided to try Lady, the dreaded peregrine. By the time all four cages were snuggled into the SUV, she turned to see Tim watching her.

Heat infused her cheeks. Despite her recent victory, she couldn't shake the shame of letting him down. Avoiding his eyes, she mumbled, "I told you I just needed some time."

"You ready to go home?" His smile broadened, melting her guilt.

"Oh yeah."

He loaded food for their guests, and they drove away from the center, barely able to see the road in front of them through the smoky beams from the headlights. But they drove out of it as they traveled up the hill to Trista's cabin.

"I called home a little while ago," he said as he turned onto the road leading to the cabin.

Glenys gasped. "Your grandfather! Is he safe?"

"Yes, but Aunt Barb moved him to her place. She said the smoke was extremely thick at my house. He's had breathing problems in the past."

"Oh, I hope he'll be okay." She bowed her head while Tim drove. "Lord, please be with Gramps tonight. Keep his breathing in check, and please keep him coherent so he won't be afraid. Also, please snuff out this fire so it does no property damage, and thank You in advance for keeping the center out of its path. In Jesus' name, amen." When she opened her eyes, Tim glanced at her with watery eyes. Had he been moved or was it the smoke?

"Thanks, that means a lot."

What could she say to that? It was the least she could do for letting him down earlier. "I'm sorry, for freezing up like I did. I really thought I could at least carry a cage. But knowing what was inside. . ."

"Hey, looks like you overcame that." He motioned to the back with his thumb. "Mandy told me you helped her load those owls. Plus you worked past your fear and picked up the carriers with Heidi and Lady inside. That's huge considering you couldn't even stand within five feet of them before."

"Well, there wasn't a piece of plastic between us then." She laughed, but her nerves made it come out as a twitter.

They pulled up her drive, and Tim cut the engine. "Looks like you ruined your dress."

She looked down at the tattered and soiled material. "Dresses can be replaced. Life can't."

His smile told her she'd given the right answer. He opened his car door and walked around to open hers. "Well, you go take a long soak and sleep well. You deserve it."

"Where are you taking the birds?" She slid out of the car, enjoying the fact that he didn't move much to get out of her way.

"I don't know yet. I can't take them home. It's still too smoky there, and Aunt Barb's place is too small."

"Leave them here."

"I'd have to stay with them. I'm fairly sure you're not at the point where you can feed them."

"We have a couch."

He glanced around nervously. "Uh, will Trista be here?"

"No, she told me she needed to go back with Vic. They'll be taking care of some eagles and vultures there. If you're worried about propriety, I'll be certain to bar my door."

That didn't seem to quench his nervousness. "I don't really have a choice, do I?"

"Not that I know of."

"Okay"—he wandered to the back of the SUV—"if you're sure your friend won't mind."

Glenys laughed. "Trista would be the last to mind."

They unloaded the birds and set the two from the outside enclosures in a protected part of the backyard. But Dunk and Lady earned places on the floor of the kitchen, where they could be kept warm. Glenys found some extra sheets and draped them over the carriers.

But when Dunk's peeps sounded unsure, Glenys lowered herself to the floor where he could see her. "So, what is the next step in his treatment?" She glanced at Tim, who offered her a fresh cup of tea and squatted near her with his own.

"His puncture wounds are healing nicely, but he lost some key feathers in the cat attack. We've saved other owl feathers and will imp them in to see if they'll help him fly."

She raised a brow. "What does that mean?"

"Graft. We take a bamboo shoot and stick it inside the shaft of the donor feather and glue it in place. Then we stick the exposed half of the shoot into the damaged shaft, also gluing it in place."

"Wow, you go to all lengths to save these guys, don't you?"

He shrugged and moved to the table. "We try."

Satisfied that Dunk felt safe now, Glenys lowered the sheet over the cage door. "I can't believe it took a near disaster to get me to move forward in my progress."

"I'm sorry I snapped your head off. Gramps was right." He rubbed the back of his neck. "I do put more stock in birds than in people."

She stood and joined him at the round pine table. With a hand on his, she looked into his eyes. "There are times when that's appropriate, and tonight was one of those times."

He flipped his hand to hold hers, and a thrill shot through her arm and burst into a fireworks display somewhere behind her rib cage.

"I was proud of you tonight." The tone of his voice, as well as his words, soothed the need to prove herself to him.

He reached toward her cheek and stroked it with his thumb. "You're wearing battle paint."

"So are you." She knew they both proudly wore smudge and grime, evidence of their hard work.

"On you it looks becoming." He leaned in as his hand slipped behind her neck. Their lips touched in a salty mix that quickly turned sweet. When they parted, he touched her forehead with his. "I had hoped to do that tonight when we weren't both a sooty mess."

"Waylaid plans, huh?"

"Yeah. Leave it to a forest fire to—" Another spontaneous kiss drew them to stand where their arms could enfold each other.

After a moment Tim pulled away first. "Okay. This is nice, but I think I'd better go sleep in my car."

Warmth rushed to Glenys's cheeks. "I hate the thought of you out there in the cold. Let me do it. I've suffered worse while on location filming a training video on winter hiking in the High Sierra."

He cupped her chin and kissed the corner of her mouth. "What kind of a gentleman would I be if I let you do that?" Pulling away, he seemed reluctant to leave. "I'll check on the outside guests first."

As she watched his retreating figure, she praised God for this man of integrity. What a story to tell Trista.

thirteen

The next morning Tim's cell phone rang, and as he answered it, his left calf cramped. He tried to stretch, but the car door prevented it. It was then he remembered he'd spent the night in the back of his SUV.

"Hi. . .ow. . .Mandy," he said as he stumbled out of the car and stomped his foot on the ground.

"Are you okay? You sound funny."

"I'm fine, just a cramp." A baseball-sized knot, to be exact. He did a lunge stretch against the side of his car, and it slowly unknotted.

"Too much activity last night? That was a lot of going up and down those hills to evacuate."

"Yeah." And a night spent in his car afterward didn't help. "What do you need? Everything okay there?"

"The fire danger has passed. I'm calling everyone to let them know it's safe to return."

"Okay, I'll get my passengers loaded back up." He didn't feel the need to tell her he'd spent the night in Glenys's driveway.

When he closed his phone, he limped to the cabin. The back door was unlocked, so Tim went inside to get Dunk and Lady, then loaded up Heidi and Oliver, a screech owl that Glenys managed to get into a cage. He was so proud of her.

Since she was still in bed, no doubt exhausted from the day before, he left a note assuring her he could handle getting all the birds where they needed to be.

At the center, Tim removed Heidi from her cage and put her back into the enclosure. As he did so, he thought about

111

the confusing events of yesterday.

Was it really just yesterday?

The outing to Oakley, where he'd convinced himself he'd only asked Glenys along as payback for her kindness to his grandfather; his conversation—and conviction—with alpaca-owner Hannie; a near-kiss with Glenys; a forest fire; and then a satisfying smooch that had him tossing and turning in the back of his uncomfortable SUV all night.

What had he done?

In daylight it all seemed clear. Glenys would leave and take his heart with him. Well, he couldn't let that happen. He'd have to resist her innocent seductiveness. Explain to her that he simply got caught up in the drama of the evening.

Then again, watching her meld into his world made him almost believe she might stay. But he couldn't ask her to give up her dream. Could he handle a long-distance relationship? With an actress?

As if on cue, he received a text from his mother.

Sorry to hear about Dad. I can't possibly get away. Important audition for margarine commercial. Give him hug from me.

"Yeah, Mom. Margarine is so much more important than your father's mental condition."

Heidi squawked from her limb as if in agreement.

He moved on to help deliver the other birds the volunteers had brought back to their homes, still mulling over his growing attraction to Glenys that overtook him nearly as fast as a forest fire. Would she leave and send back these kinds of texts? *Sorry, darling, but audition for greeting card company is more important than us being together. I'll mail you a hug, because I care enough to send the best. Please share it with Gramps.*

A shudder rattled his bones. Best to put their relationship back on a purely platonic level. If not for himself, then certainly for Gramps. He didn't need one more person letting him down.

Throughout the day, he worked at getting all the residents back into their enclosures as people brought them in, but his mind stayed on Glenys. He resolved to keep his distance emotionally, but when Glenys showed up to check on Dunk, her attention to the little bird endeared her to Tim all the more.

"I'm sorry I missed you this morning," she said as he joined her. "I would have made you breakfast."

Tim quickly looked around to be sure no one overheard their conversation. He didn't want anyone to get the wrong idea.

"I think the outing did him good." She peered at Dunk through the metal bars of the cage door. "His eyes are alert."

She replaced Dunk's sheet over the cage so he could rest, then turned to Tim. "About last night—"

Tim took a deep breath. "You're right. It was too fast. And you're leaving. So why pursue a relationship? Somebody will only get hurt."

The pain in her eyes stopped his runaway words. "I was going to say thank you for the wonderful evening—before *and* after the fire."

"I'm sorry." Tim pried his foot out of his mouth. "Can we start over? Things just happened kinda fast last night."

She pinched her lips, but appeared to think about it. Finally, she nodded. "That's a good idea. Let's maintain a professional relationship for now."

He caved to the lower lip that barely pouted. "No. Let's go back to a special friendship and see where that leads, okay?"

"Okay." Her dimple deepened. "Then back to the matters at hand. I love working with the owls, but I'm not getting much exposure to the falcons."

"I have an idea." He walked her out of the clinic into the chilly autumn air. She pulled her jacket closed, and he resisted the urge to put his arm around her. "Would you be able to come earlier and catch me before I leave for the day? Follow me around during the feeding?"

The sparkle returned to her eyes. "I could definitely do that." She shivered slightly. "I'm glad I'll be going home before winter hits. I already miss my California sunshine."

Well, that nailed that dream inside the coffin.

As she left him to enter the visitor center, his cell phone chirped. It was Aunt Barb.

"Hi, Auntie. Are you on the way to Gramps's doctor appointment?"

"No, Tim. Listen. We're not at the clinic, we're at the hospital."

Tim's heart thudded with the rhythm of a sledgehammer. "What happened?"

"The smoke last night kicked off his emphysema. It started this morning and looked to be only a temporary attack, but he's really struggling to breathe. They'll probably admit him."

"I'll be there as soon as I can."

Glenys came out carrying her purse. She must have read the alarm on his face. "What's wrong?"

"Gramps is in the hospital. An emphysema attack."

"Let's go." She started to walk away from him.

"Wait." He grabbed her forearm and turned her away from the parking lot. "You don't need to put your life on hold again for my family problems."

Concern snuffed the sparkle from her eyes. "I love your grandfather. But if you'd rather I not go, I respect that. I guess I've been horning in on your personal life lately. I'll just go home and pray for him."

She started to walk away, a dejected slump to her shoulders. Tim couldn't leave her thinking she wasn't welcome. "Would it mean that much to you?"

She swiveled to face him, a smile blossoming on her face. "In and out. Just long enough to let him know I care. Then I'll sit in the waiting room and leave you two alone together."

He threw his arm over her shoulders, buddy style. "Come on, Sunshine. You'd probably do him a lot of good."

He offered to drive and bring her back to her car since they had to go into Merrick. Once they were on their way, he regretted that decision. Lavender scent reached up his nostrils and dulled the common sense lobe of his brain.

To get his mind off the unpretentious, un-actressy person sitting next to him, he asked her to pray aloud for his grandfather. "He brought this illness on himself from years of smoking, but he quit after Gram died."

She bowed her head and said a heartfelt, Spirit-led prayer that brought a lump to Tim's throat.

"Thank you."

This woman was nothing like his mother. Her actress friend was though, and Tim said a silent prayer of his own that Glenys wouldn't be influenced.

When they arrived at the hospital, Tim and Glenys walked into Gramps's room, where he lay on his back with a tube running oxygen into his nose. Aunt Barb rose from the one chair. "He's been sleeping off and on since they admitted him. Poor thing was probably worn out after our adventure yesterday."

Tim offered Glenys the chair and stood by his grandfather's bedside. "He looks so frail. When did he get so old?"

Aunt Barb stretched her back and looked as though she needed a break. "Seems all of a sudden, doesn't it?"

Gramps's eyes fluttered open, and his gaze rested on Glenys. "Libby?"

"No, Gramps, this isn't Mom." He wanted to shout at his grandfather, tell him to stop getting old.

Glenys pulled the elderly hand into hers, neither denying nor confirming. Just smiling.

"Oh. Timmy's girl." He smiled back and waggled her hand in his.

A pink blush bloomed on Glenys's face. "How are you feeling?"

"Oh"—he shook his head—"so much fuss over an old man with a cough. I'll be outta here tomorrow."

"You need to take care of yourself. I would be very sad if anything happened to you."

Gramps let go of her hand and brushed her cheek with a knuckle, her flawless skin contrasting with his age spots.

She started to rise, apparently to fulfill her "in and out" rule, but Tim suddenly couldn't bear the thought of her not being there. He placed a hand on her shoulder, and she relaxed back into the chair.

Gramps drifted off again. Tim looked at Glenys. "We'll be right back." He motioned to Aunt Barb, and she followed him out of the room. They wandered to a waiting area where they both sat on purple vinyl couches. The entire area had been decorated in bright, cheery colors.

"I didn't want to talk in front of Gramps. Mom texted me today."

"I know, she did me, too. I called her right away, but it went to voice mail. She's avoiding us."

Tim leaned on his elbows and rubbed his eyes. "You know. I'm at the point where I say cut her loose. She doesn't care about us. Why should we care about her?"

He felt his aunt's hand on his shoulder. "That's anger talking, not the Lord. I've had those thoughts plenty of times, but I'm always convicted. As long as we're able to connect with her, I feel I need to continue to reach out to her."

Tim suddenly remembered his conversation with the owner of the alpaca ranch. He told his aunt about her. "She hadn't been much different than Mom. Both went their own ways, leaving behind people who loved them. But God reached Hannie."

"God can reach your mother, too. I believe that with all my

heart." Pain laced the faith he saw in her eyes. "I have to."

As they returned to the room, a sweet soprano voice drifted into the corridor, getting louder until Tim realized it was Glenys singing "I've Got a Crush on You." Gramps lay with his eyes closed, but a smile curved his lips. She stopped when they entered.

"How do you know the words to that song?" Tim marveled at this woman's versatility.

"Puh-lease. Everyone in the entertainment industry should know Gershwin. Gramps was telling me about his days spent with the Berlin Airlift back in the forties, and the conversation moved naturally to the hit parade."

A nurse came in and checked Gramps's vitals. Once she assured them he would rest comfortably for the night, Aunt Barb volunteered to stay at the hospital so Tim could take Glenys back.

He lost another piece of his heart to her when she bent and placed a kiss on the wrinkled forehead.

As they drove home, Tim's baffled emotions threatened to overcome him. His own mother couldn't give them the time of day, and the woman sitting next to him, whom he didn't want to become involved with, had apparently adopted his family.

I don't know what You're doing to me, Lord. Do You like me off-balance like this? He shouldn't have asked the question, because he felt that deep down, off-balance was exactly where God wanted him. Was God about to topple his world?

Glenys smiled at him from the passenger seat, the dimple acting as a pawn in God's master plan.

I'm in so much trouble.

fourteen

By Tuesday all was back to normal at the center. When Glenys showed up an hour early, as Tim had suggested, she looked for him in the visitor center.

"May I help you, sweetheart?"

"Hi, Cyrano. Tim around?"

"Around. . .Tim."

"Why do I bother asking you questions when your answers are never in the right order?"

"Order. . .Tim around."

Glenys chuckled. "Maybe you do know what you're saying."

"Dimple."

Her hand flew to her cheek. "Who is talking about my dimple?" Then again, there could be other people with dimples, or they could have been discussing dimples on a golf ball.

"Cute dimple."

Maybe not. She had no time to figure it out. She needed to find Tim. As she walked out, she found herself scrutinizing everybody's faces looking for dimples. From Mandy and Camille, who were cleaning up after a school talk, to a couple of women volunteers she barely knew. Of course, it didn't help if they weren't smiling. Maybe she should walk around with a funny face to see who she could get to laugh.

She lost interest in the dimple search when she saw Vic and Trista at the vulture cage. She shuddered. A vulture would be one bird she'd never handle.

She waved and joined them. "Feeling better, Vic?" He didn't have the pasty pallor he had the day before.

"Much. I had a great nurse." He winked at Trista.

"And is she still needed?" Glenys pinched her lips shut, but too late. The snide remark had already escaped.

"I'm sorry I haven't been home lately." At least Trista had the courtesy to look apologetic.

"Me, too. I was looking forward to some girl time." She pinned Vic with a look, hoping he'd get the hint and back off from pursuing her friend. The vultures looked down on them from their perch, leaving Glenys with an uneasy feeling. Were they waiting for her to kick the bucket?

"You're right." Trista laid a hand on Vic's arm, almost comforting him. "Vic's better now, so I'll be home tonight. Is that okay, hon?" She asked permission? What was happening between these two?

Vic slipped his fingers in his front pockets and drew his shoulders to his neck. "Am I going to live?"

Trista nodded and kissed his cheek.

He sighed heavily. "Then fine. I can suffer for the sake of friendship."

"Are you busy," Glenys asked Trista, "or can you walk with me while I look for Tim?"

"I'm done for the day." She brushed Vic's hand with the back of hers.

Yep. Glenys needed to nip that in the bud.

As they walked away, Glenys shoved her hands into her jacket pockets. "I thought you were going to quit volunteering here."

Trista glanced over her shoulder at Vic. "I was persuaded to stay."

"Do you know what you're doing, Tris?" She jerked her head in Vic's general direction.

Trista blushed. Glenys had never seen that before. "I like him, Glen. You've been wrong about him."

"I hope so. But I don't want you to get hurt."

"Don't worry. I know what I'm doing."

Tim came walking around the corner with Heidi on his hand. Glenys had made some progress it was true, but the sudden appearance was still a shock. She put Trista between herself and Tim.

"I've been looking for you," both Tim and Glenys said together.

Trista pulled away. "Vic is taking me to dinner, but I promise I'll see you at home tonight."

When she was out of hearing range, Tim spoke in a near whisper.

"I've heard the other women talking. They said Vic hasn't been hitting on them lately. I thought it was because he was sick, but maybe it's because he has a girl now."

"Bite your tongue. Trista doesn't need someone like Vic. I'd rather she found a nice man with morals. A Christian man who will take care of her. Someone like—"

He raised an eyebrow, apparently waiting for her to continue.

"Never mind." She'd almost said someone like Tim.

"Okay. Staying out of that one. You know her better than I do. But it seems if someone is influencing Vic to behave himself, that might be a good thing."

She didn't want to get into it either. "So, are we working with Heidi?" She pointed to the bird on his hand.

"Yes. The center has been booked for a Raptor Reading on Friday. I thought we'd rehearse. We'll work in the visitor center since it's nippy out here."

"Do we need to cover Cyrano? Hawks and parrots don't mix, do they?"

"No, but these two have worked together a lot. Both are old hats at what they do in the bird theater world."

They entered the building, and Tim disappeared in a back room with Heidi. "I'll go find a T stand."

Glenys waited near Cyrano's playpen. He cocked his head in an impossible bend.

"Sweetheart? Dimple?"

Tim reentered, dragging a carpeted wooden perch behind him. He placed Heidi on it, then he pulled a children's book off a shelf.

"This is what we'll be reading."

She thumbed through it. "This is cute. I like the little old lady." She laughed at the stooped gray-haired woman who owned a bird.

"We usually just read, show the pictures, and have the bird sitting on the perch. Then we tell the kids some facts and go home. But it will be more interesting if you acted it out. It will only be effective if you're able to hold the bird. You want to try?"

"You're a sneaky man, Tim Vogel. Combining my passion with my fear."

An evil grin appeared on his face. "Hey, it was Vic's idea. We'll see if it works."

He handed her a stuffed toy bird so she could get down her part. "Pretend you're Mrs. Hawk. She loves her bird. And more than that, she trusts her bird."

"Well, look at her." Glenys pointed to the cover. "She doesn't have to worry about the bird gouging her eyes out."

Tim examined the artist's rendering. "Why not?"

"Because she has thick glasses."

He laughed, a hearty sound that made her want to make him laugh more often. "Then we'll get you glasses." As Tim read the story *Mrs. Hawk and Her Hawk*, Glenys pantomimed. It had been awhile since she performed, and she soaked in the movements, not realizing how thirsty she'd been for something familiar.

Tim's reading had her laughing, especially when his voice went falsetto to sound like the elderly Mrs. Hawk. Finally, after a particularly long giggling session, he asked, "Do you think I should let you say the lines?"

"Oh no, this will have the kids rolling on the floor."

He put down the book and stood, then grasped her shoulders and turned her toward Heidi. "Time to try this for real."

She donned a glove with a shaky hand, but relaxed as she concentrated on Tim standing behind her, protecting her if need be. With his hand on her left shoulder, he took her right elbow and straightened her arm. "Just like the canaries and the owls. You can do this."

Heidi glared at her, as if asking who she thought she was to approach her in such a manner.

"Heidi hates me."

"No she doesn't. She just needs to know that you won't drop her. You must appear more confident."

"Even if I'm not feeling it?"

"Yes. You'll become more comfortable the more you do this. Remember my canaries? You did great with them, eventually. And what about Dunk? Now you can not only handle him but all the other owls here."

"Not the great horned owl."

"I admit, his size is daunting, but I have no doubt you'll be able to work with him soon."

His confidence buoyed her resolve. "Okay, let's do this."

She held her hand near Heidi's feet. Listening to Mrs. Hawk's dialogue as Tim read, she took on her character and found the strength she needed. Heidi stepped onto her hand, and Glenys clipped the leash to the jesses and wound them in her palm. "I'm doing it." She whispered the words, afraid that by saying them out loud the whole experience would dissolve.

Tim interrupted his reading and also whispered, "Great job."

After finishing the rest of the piece, he said, "Now, take her back to the perch."

Glenys allowed Heidi to step onto the perch and unclipped

the leash. "I did it." She wanted to shout, but certainly didn't want to spook Heidi. In her quiet exuberance, she swiveled right into Tim's arms.

He hugged her tight. "I'm so proud of you."

She leaned her head back to search his brown-gold eyes. "Thank you for your patience."

"Super-human patience," he corrected.

"It wasn't that bad."

"Yes it was. It was very bad."

As they stood holding each other and gazing into each other's eyes, Glenys felt the same magnetic pull as their first kiss just two days prior. Inches from his lips, she closed her eyes, anticipation zinging through her like love arrows.

But then his arms dropped, and he backed away. Confusion dissolved the arrows.

"I guess you'll be leaving soon then." A bitter tone laced his words.

This confused her even more. He knew she'd be leaving eventually, but it needn't be good-bye forever.

"I still have to handle the peregrine, but yes. Thanks to you."

"Yeah. Thanks to me."

"I still have a little time. I'd like to do something special for you and Gramps before I go."

He backed up, bumping Cyrano's playpen. "I don't know. We'll see."

They continued to rehearse the story, and this time she held Heidi with more confidence. But the fun had been sucked from the room.

"I think you have it now. You probably have work to do, and I need to get Heidi back to her enclosure." He left abruptly, leaving Glenys with Cyrano.

"Dimple. Green eyes. Pretty." The bird started in again with insistence.

"Okay, Cyrano. I'm getting that someone is talking about me."

"Tim. Around."

She gave him a treat, and he peered at it as if she'd given him a spider to eat. Finally, he nibbled at it.

"Birds." She shook her head. "What are you thinking?"

fifteen

What was I thinking? Falling for an actress?

Tim drove home with Cyrano chattering from his cage in the backseat. With the cover muffling the sound, he could only make out certain words, like his name along with "order" and "around." He wondered if Glenys had said this and was tired of being ordered around.

Well, that would stop soon enough. She'd graduated to holding a hawk. Soon she'd be able to handle the peregrine falcon, and then she would leave. He couldn't bear a long-distance relationship, not after his mother had disappointed him so many times.

He pulled into his drive, then unloaded Cyrano and took him into the house.

Gramps sat in his easy chair looking weary after his latest adventure. Before being released from the hospital that morning, Gramps's doctor kept their appointment and paid him a visit. Tim told him about the trips down memory lane that seemed too real, and the doctor agreed Gramps should be evaluated. After learning that the lack of oxygen from emphysema could mask dementia symptoms, Tim promised to make another appointment after Gramps recovered.

Tim had brought him home afterward, but Aunt Barb had agreed to sit with him while Tim went to work. When he arrived home, she was just putting supper on the table.

"You don't have to cook for us." He pecked a kiss on his aunt's head.

"It's no trouble. I'm here anyway."

"Thanks for being here today." He noted her tired eyes. She

wasn't used to watching an old man during her downtime.

She glanced into the living room where Gramps watched Cyrano on the side table entertaining him. "He's my father." Her eyes suddenly misted. "And I don't know how long he'll remember me."

Tim ushered her to the table and pulled out a chair for her, then sat next to her. "Let's wait and see what his doctor says. Could be a special diet might help. I've read they've done wonders through research in coming up with alternatives. And, of course, we'll pray."

She placed the palm of her hand on his cheek. "Why couldn't you have been mine? My sister doesn't deserve a son like you." Her bitterness created an ache in the pit of Tim's stomach. "She had you, and I was left childless."

"I had no idea you felt this way. I'm so sorry you and Uncle Mack didn't have children before he died. You've made a great surrogate mom through the years, though. Gramps and I could never have survived without you."

Love poured from her eyes, along with an errant tear. "Thank you, Timmy." She swiped the tear away with a finger. "I don't know what's wrong with me lately. I guess it just breaks my heart that your grandfather may never see his daughter again."

"I'll do what I can to get her to visit."

She sat with her arms folded, and her mouth turned down, looking very much like Gramps during his stubborn moments.

"Okay?" he prompted as he sat in her line of vision. If she would just look at him, she would come back from this mood she was in.

Finally, a small grin played in the corner of her mouth.

"That's my girl. Let's keep giving her updates as his condition changes. Maybe she'll come around." Well, probably not, but at least it made his aunt feel better.

"Hey"—she hopped up, once again the "mom" taking care

of her boys—"this soup is getting cold. Call your grandfather in while I slice some bread." She stopped and looked at him in her bustling. "Did I ever tell you you're my favorite nephew?"

He chuckled. "I'm your only nephew."

&

Glenys finished her shift and left for the cabin, still confused over Tim's hasty departure earlier that evening. They had shared a kiss after the forest fire, but then he turned on her like a wild hawk.

When she arrived home, she was happy to see Trista's car in the drive, but disheartened to see Vic's there as well. When Glenys had said she wanted girl time, she thought Trista had gotten the hint.

Inside the house, Trista and Vic sat on the couch watching a movie. An innocent scene until Glenys took it in fully. The left side of Trista's blouse hung out sloppily, and Vic's shirt was buttoned crooked.

She mumbled a greeting to their hearty hellos, then headed straight for her room. After dragging her suitcase from the closet, she started pitching her clothes inside.

"What are you doing?" Trista stood at the bedroom door, her eyes wide.

"I think I should go to a hotel. I'm obviously a third wheel here."

"No you're not." Trista shouldered Glenys out of the way and proceeded to unpack the suitcase, tossing underwear and nightclothes back into the drawer. Then she whirled on Glenys. "Are you jealous?"

An inappropriate guffaw escaped Glenys's throat. "You can't be serious."

"Why else would you be upset?"

"Do you think I have feelings for that. . ."—she pointed to the now-closed door, but aimed at Vic on the other side—"predator out there?"

Trista's eyes went even wider than before. "No, I hadn't even thought of that."

"Then what do you mean?" Glenys, suddenly weary, plopped into the small armchair near her window.

"I'm talking about me. You're jealous that Vic is taking me away from you."

"Don't be absurd." But how close did that hit the mark? Was he a falcon come to scoop her dear friend away, and possibly away from the moral foundation Glenys had been trying to build? If so, then jealousy wasn't the right word. Anger summed it up better.

Glenys leaned on her knees and pressed her fists into her temples. "Can't you see him for who he is?"

Trista bristled. "Can't you?"

Glenys's head jerked up. "He's a womanizer, Trista. He doesn't care at all about anyone but himself."

"That's an act, Glen." Trista lowered her voice and glanced toward the closed door. "He's really very insecure around women. That's why he talks big."

"And you know this how?"

"He told me."

Glenys must have looked skeptical.

Trista continued to defend Vic. "Think about it. Why would a man as you portray him admit to that? He said he rarely lets people in because he's an introvert."

Glenys snorted. "Really? He used that word?"

"I'm serious. And if you weren't so busy judging him, you'd see that for yourself." After a long moment of silence, Trista said, "I have an idea. He wants to take me rafting this weekend. Why don't I ask if you can come along? You can invite Tim, and we'll make it a foursome. Then you can see Vic the way I see him."

Could Glenys handle a whole day of Vic's chauvinism? She nearly said no, but Trista's entreating eyes broke her down. "Fine. I'll call Tim, but after the way he acted today, I'm not sure he wants to go anywhere with me."

"Why? What happened?"

"I don't know. We were rehearsing a story that we're going to present to a school, I held a hawk—"

"You held a hawk?" Trista clapped her hands lightly. "Congratulations!"

"Thanks, but it seems a hollow victory. After our hug—"

"You hugged?" Now Trista's mouth lay open.

"Will you let me finish?"

Trista sat back and clamped her lips shut, but her eyes danced.

"After our hug and near-kiss—"

"What? Maybe you'd better start over."

Glenys left out the telling of their first kiss, choosing to relish it a little longer. But she related what had happened just an hour before without any interruptions.

"You know why Tim acted that way, don't you?" Trista put on a Lucy, the psychiatrist, U-shaped smile to Glenys's dim Charlie Brown.

"He hates me?"

"How can you be so smart, yet so dumb? Now that you're accomplishing the thing that brought you here, you'll be leaving."

"So he wants to drive me away?"

"In a sense, yes." Trista reached out and shook Glenys's wrist. "You goof. He's in love with you. But you're about to leave him, so he's pulling a protective shell around himself."

A warm, toasty feeling came over Glenys as if she'd just stepped into the light of a campfire on a chilly night. "Then I'll talk to Tim tomorrow. I think a day on the river would do him good."

❧

Saturday afternoon Tim drove up the highway and located the parking area near the reservoir dam where the Rogue

River spilled out and continued on to the ocean. He almost stayed home. How did he get talked into rafting with the three people he most wanted to avoid?

The dimple.

If Glenys had called instead of accosting him with that beautiful smile, he might have been able to say no. Instead, here he was, dressed to get doused with chilly river water and waving at the two actresses and Vic.

"I'm so happy you decided to join us." Glenys bounced over to him, with a sparkle in her eyes that he hadn't seen before.

"Yeah. Well. . .thanks for inviting me."

Vic slapped him on the back. "I'm glad you're here, old man." He glanced at the women. "Not that I couldn't handle two girls."

Glenys rolled her eyes—Tim's sentiments exactly.

The raft had already been inflated.

"Is all this equipment yours?" Tim asked as Vic handed him a plastic helmet, orange life vest, and paddle.

"Yeah. I used to be a guide."

This guy was full of surprises—the first allowing two extra people to invade his date with Trista.

He proceeded to lay out the ground rules. "This will be a gentle thirteen-mile ride with twenty-three rapids. Don't worry, though, none is considered over a Class II. We still must maintain safety, though. Tim, you told me you've rafted before, right?"

"A couple of times."

"Then I'll sit in the back since I'm most experienced. You sit in front and help steer. We'll put the two ladies in the middle. Use your paddles the way I just showed you, but really, all you have to do is hang on and look pretty."

Trista blushed a rosy pink, but Glenys jutted out her chin, looking indignant. Her friend pulled her to the raft before the words piling up behind her pinched lips spilled out.

"So," Tim said as he stepped into the raft, "how are we getting back to get our cars?"

"I left my Excursion in Shady Pine. After we dock, we'll load the raft on it and I'll drive us all back."

They each donned their helmets, gripped their yellow paddles by the blue handles, and shoved off. Tim felt Glenys's presence behind him. She and Trista sat side by side in the middle. He glanced over his left shoulder, and her smile made him look forward to the whole uncomfortable day.

The water soon buoyed them, and they floated away. Tim began to relax as he dipped his paddle into the current. There was something cathartic about rivers. Their gentle flow, the beautiful scenery. The giggles coming from the middle of the raft.

Concentrate, Vogel. It wouldn't do to capsize the vessel because of the tinkling laughter that relentlessly tickled his ear.

He also heard Vic talking to Trista and noted that he didn't speak to her the way he did the women at the center.

"You doing okay there, hon?"

"Yes, darling."

"Comfortable?"

"Very, knowing you're in control."

At times he wondered if someone had tossed Vic from the boat and replaced him with a kinder, gentler clone.

After an exhilarating ride, they reached a place mid-trip where Vic suggested they rest. He'd brought food, so they pulled the raft onto dry land and unstrapped the cooler. The edge of the raft served as a bench while they ate sandwiches and drank flavored sports water.

Glenys sat so near to Tim that their knees brushed. He wanted to shift away, but something anchored him to the spot. He realized after a moment it was her very presence that made him reluctant to move. No lingering lavender, no dimple, just Glenys.

This thought was disconcerting and exhilarating at the same time.

Vic's voice pulled him from his analyzing. He praised everyone for a fine job and warned them of white water ahead. That's exactly how Tim felt. His heart was headed into rough white water, and he didn't even have a paddle to steer clear.

Glenys finished her sandwich and took a sip of her water. She glanced at Trista, but directed her comment to Tim. "I'm looking forward to church tomorrow. Your pastor is so funny and entertaining."

Tim cocked a brow at her. Not only was her subject change abrupt, but he wouldn't call Pastor Rick entertaining. Sure, he knew how to tell a joke, but it was hardly nonstop as Glenys tried to make it sound. She motioned with her eyes to Trista. Perhaps signaling him? Was she trying to make the Sunday service sound exciting to the nonchurchgoer?

Vic was the one to pipe in. "You know, Tim, I've been thinking. After nearly losing the center to fire, you really kept your head." He toed a small pinecone that had fallen into the raft. "I heard about the prayer you said for me before everyone helped evacuate. Might be why I began to feel well enough to help. It touched me."

Tim marveled at the way God worked.

Glenys stared at Vic, her jaw dusting the ground. Tim checked his as well to see if it had also dropped. Now he was sure someone had replaced the real Vic.

Glenys recovered first. "Vic, would you like to come to church with us tomorrow? No obligation."

Vic glanced at Trista, who had been quiet during the conversation. She now glared at Glenys. Finally, after an awkward moment of silence, Vic spoke. "Yes. I'd like to go. My folks used to take me, and I'd attend Sunday school. I kinda liked it." He shrugged and glanced down at his feet.

"But after they split up, that all stopped."

"How old were you?" Glenys asked.

"Eleven." He stood to collect their trash in a plastic bag and then shoved it into the cooler.

"How tragic."

"Yeah. I lived in two households until I moved out. Dad was always trying to make me macho and told me church was for weaklings."

Vic stood in silence for a moment longer than seemed comfortable. Tim sensed he needed to move on from that revealing statement. "You know, if you were a jock in school, we never would have gotten along. I was a science nerd."

Vic's mouth worked in a tense line. "That's the thing. I was a skinny geek myself." He pulled the strap tight around the cooler and grabbed his helmet. "Man, I don't know why I just confessed that." He began to drag the raft back to the water, and Tim grabbed a handle to help.

"Maybe we'd have gotten along after all," Tim said.

"I found out early on that I could get myself out of most any situation with a smile. The girls loved me." He wiggled his eyebrows as he helped the women step into the raft.

And there was Vic's defense mechanism. Having this brief glimpse into the man's past helped Tim know how to pray for him and how to interact with him at the center.

Tim and Glenys exchanged looks. He wondered if she felt as he had, that he'd misjudged Vic.

Despite Vic's flirting, Trista's face remained deadpan. A few strategic glares in Glenys's direction showed where Trista directed her anger. But as she settled into the raft, she lifted her paddle over her head and said, "Hey, we're getting too serious. I'm here to have fun. Let's go."

Vic glanced at his watch. "You're right. We don't want to be caught on the river after dark."

They finished the last leg of their trip, Vic and Glenys

chatting during the slower flow of the river. But Trista's silence lay heavy in the raft. When he glanced over his shoulder, she sat straight, gripping the paddle as if fearing it would slip away.

Ice formed inside Vic's car on the ride back. Was Trista jealous that Vic and Glenys were hitting it off? No, if she were jealous, she'd probably be hanging on Vic, trying to gain back his attention. She was clearly angry with both Vic and Glenys over something.

After they arrived back at the parking area, Trista headed straight for her car without saying a word.

"There goes my ride," Glenys said while shaking her head at the retreating vehicle.

"I'll take you back." Tim turned to thank Vic for the day. "I had a great time. We should do it again."

Vic smiled back and shook Tim's hand. "Yeah, me, too. I guess we never got a chance to know each other at the center. This was a good thing."

Yes it was. Too good. Now Tim didn't have a nemesis, and he was more attracted to the actress than ever before.

Glenys told Vic when and where church was. When she joined Tim in his SUV, she grinned, then leaned her head back and sighed.

"Why are you smiling?" Tim pulled onto the road. "It looks like your friend has a beef with you."

"She's not happy that Vic is coming to church with us."

"Really? That's why?" He glanced again at Glenys's serene face in the evening glow. "And you're happy about that?"

She nodded. "If Vic comes, I'm certain he'll get her to go. I've invited her I don't know how many times."

She glanced his way. "Thanks for joining us today. I was afraid you'd turn me down."

He shifted in his seat. "Gramps asked about you today. I've been trying to let him know that you'll be leaving soon. He asked if I'd invite you to his birthday party this Monday. It's his eightieth, so my aunt and I want to make it special for him."

In the waning light as dusk settled in, a pink glow dusted her cheeks, rivaling the sunset. "I'd like that."

He'd like that, too. And after he dropped her off, he would go home and tell Cyrano that he would give her reasons to want to stay in Shady Pine with Gramps. . .and Aunt Barb. . . and with him.

sixteen

"I can't believe you asked him to church." Trista whirled on Glenys before she could shut the front door.

"No, I'm sure you could believe that. What you can't believe is that he accepted. Why aren't you angry with Vic?"

"I am, but. . ."

Glenys waited, knowing Trista had no more excuses. She put down her purse and led Trista to the sofa. "Look, come with us or don't. I'll never stop hoping. But don't begrudge Vic for wanting to fill a need."

"He'll change." Trista pressed a fist into the arm of the couch.

"He'll grow. Why do you care if he goes to church? You never minded me going, and we've been friends for several years."

"Because I don't want to marry you."

"Marry?" Glenys picked her jaw up off the floor for the second time that day. "You barely know this guy."

"But we're soul mates. If he gets religion, we won't have anything in common."

"You have plenty in common that 'getting religion' won't change. And besides, it's just one day. You're acting like he'll come to church and then join a monastery."

Her eyes grew wide. "I hadn't even thought of that." She thrust her face into her hands.

Glenys chuckled and hugged her friend. "Relax. We don't have monasteries in our denomination."

Trista mumbled something behind her hands.

"What was that?" Glenys continued to rock and comfort her friend.

"I said, I'll go."

Glenys wanted to hop around the room and celebrate, but instead squeezed Trista a little harder.

The next day, Glenys sat in the kitchen reading her Bible while waiting on Trista. It had been tough to coax her friend out of bed that early. Glenys feared she might dig in and refuse to go, but she finally dragged herself to the shower. When she didn't show up for breakfast, Glenys checked on her.

Trista's bed had completely disappeared and was now covered with her entire wardrobe. "I don't have anything to wear," she wailed as she frantically held up one outfit after another.

Glenys looked at her watch. "If you don't choose something, it won't matter. We need to leave in twenty minutes."

She soon saw the dilemma. Trista's clothes were not appropriate for church. The skirts were too short, and the blouses too low cut.

"I have something you can wear." Glenys headed for her own room. She quickly found a navy blue shift dress. When she reentered the other bedroom, she held it out. "You're smaller than I am, but I think it will work with a belt."

Trista reached for the dress, then sank onto the bed. "What am I doing?"

Dread seized Glenys. She knelt in front of her. "I know you're not comfortable with this, but it's only one day, two hours tops. But"—she tried to swallow what she was about to say, but knew she had to say it—"if you truly are this miserable, maybe you shouldn't go."

Trista's eyes filled with tears. "Are you giving up on me?"

"Whoa! I will never give up on you." Now Glenys didn't know what to do. Should she continue to push and possibly alienate her best friend or back off and hurt her feelings? "I'm saying this is your decision. You know I love you. You know God loves you—I've told you that enough. He wants to have a relationship with you, but you must open yourself to that, just as you would with anybody else."

"That's just it. I've never had a 'relationship.'" She stressed the word, as if it were hard to say. "I've had flings. And that's what Vic started out to be. But when he got sick, something changed. Between us and inside of me." She shrugged one shoulder. "And that was startling enough, but then when he said he wanted to go to church. . .did you know he talked about it on the phone for an hour last night? It's like, after all he's gone through in the past, he's using it—"

"Like a lighthouse in a storm?"

"Yes." Trista twisted the bottom corner of her robe around her finger.

"I love that analogy. You know about my family's lighthouse in Crossroads Bay. It's been that to many people."

A frown took over Trista's face. "I guess I'm in a storm, too, but mine didn't start until just a few days ago."

"No. You've been in a storm for a long time, but you became so comfortable in it you hardly noticed. All those times you called me when you'd had too much to drink. . .all the times I had to talk you down after the tabloids tore you to shreds. . .all the times you felt lonely when no man was in your life and you called me for some girl time. . .that's when you were looking for a lighthouse in the storm, and you mistakenly thought it was me."

Trista lifted sad eyes. "And you kept trying to point me to God."

"The real Light. The only one who could save you."

Trista cast the dress aside and flung herself into Glenys's arms. They both stood and hugged while Trista poured out her heart. "You're right. I've been miserable. I only pretend to be having a great time. But with you I can be real. And I felt that with Vic, too."

Glenys pulled away to look into Trista's puffy, tear-stained eyes. "You can be real with God, too. He made you. He knows everything about you and loves you anyway."

Trista wiped her face with her fingers and sniffled. "I look a mess, but I don't care." She snatched the dress and went into her bathroom.

Glenys felt the first rays dawn onto Trista's new life.

Before long they drove to the church, and Glenys steered the car into the parking lot where she spotted Vic near the entrance with Tim. Relief flooded her. Trista wouldn't back out if Vic were there.

The blue dress trimmed Trista's already petite size. She wore a white floppy hat and large sunglasses, but without the wild party clothes or red carpet bling, she looked more beautiful than Glenys ever remembered.

Vic must have thought so, too. He didn't wait for her to walk across the graveled lot, but rushed to her side and offered a modest kiss.

Glenys caught Tim's eye and his subtle thumbs-up gesture. It felt great to share this moment with him.

Inside, they slid into a pew that Gramps was holding for them—Tim leading the way with Glenys beside him, then Trista, and on the end, Vic. Trista slipped her arm through Glenys's as if she were afraid she might be whisked off into a cult, but Glenys pressed the elbow to her side to reassure her.

Both Vic and Trista made it through the music, although it was apparent they didn't know the songs. However, Vic belted them once he learned the words. Barely a sound came from Trista's lips. Glenys knew this girl was not afraid to croon at the top of her lungs when the mood struck. But this was a different Trista standing beside her. No doubt the real Trista, sans the cloak of celebrity.

Ironically—or was it God?—the sermon that morning was on fear. The pastor spoke on allowing fear to rule instead of the Lord.

"Consider this verse from Psalm 34:4: 'I sought the LORD, and he answered me; he delivered me from all my fears.'"

It hit Glenys hard. She realized that by allowing fear to take precedence, she had shoved God aside. Suddenly she felt like a hypocrite.

After praying silently for forgiveness, peace drifted into Glenys's heart like a butterfly seeking a soft place to land. No more fear. No more running and screaming. The phobia had skittered away knowing there was no room for it.

Even if she'd been healed, Glenys realized she wanted to stay and learn more about the fascinating creatures she had so long avoided. Sadness overwhelmed her as she realized she didn't have much time left in Shady Pine.

The pastor quoted one last verse from his anointed arsenal, this time from Proverbs. " 'Fear of man will prove to be a snare, but whoever trusts in the LORD is kept safe.'"

Glenys gasped. That was the verse she'd quoted to Trista during her stalker scare. Was she listening? Perhaps hearing it from someone else would make it sink in. She risked a glance in Trista's direction. Her eyes were closed.

Listen to the Lord, Trista. God, please get through to her.

When he was finished, the pastor gave an altar call to anyone who wanted to shed their past fears and grasp God's hand for the first time in their lives.

A stirring to her right caught her attention. Vic had stood and was heading down the aisle. Had he just shed a fear? His father perhaps? Glenys felt Tim's hand slip into hers, and together they raised their joined palms in tribute to their God of the impossible.

But there was one other soul in turmoil that needed her attention. Trista sat on her hands, watching Vic, the longing in her eyes evident.

Glenys put her arm around the slender shoulders. "God's grace is free, Trista. It can't be bought by your famous director father. It won't run away like the men in your life. It addresses the issue with your stalker. Just like the pastor quoted, fear of man is a snare, but if you trust the Lord, He will keep you safe."

Trista turned large, tear-filled eyes to her.

"I know you came here to run away." Glenys swept a hair from Trista's moist face. "All that talk about wanting to show your dedication because of me was transparent."

"But I do admire you."

Glenys smiled. "But that's not what drove you here. I wanted to believe you had blown off the released stalker, but deep down, you were hurting."

"I'm sorry." The dark tresses fell into her face as she bowed her head. "I used you."

Glenys pulled her into a fierce hug. "No, I was that lighthouse that we talked about. But now"—she pointed to the front where Vic was on his knees with several people gathered—"you know who the real lighthouse is. I can't do anything for you, but God can."

Trista watched the pastor go to each person and pray. Finally, she stood.

When Glenys started to join her, joy springing from her place of hope, Trista stopped her. "I have to do this on my own."

Through a mist of tears, Glenys watched her best friend join the last man she thought would accept Christ. Trista lowered herself next to Vic, humbling herself for the first time ever.

"God is good," Tim whispered in her ear.

"All the time," she whispered back.

He put his arm around her and kissed her head. Despite her joy of the moment, she suddenly felt sad. The days were soaring by, and she longed to stay in his embrace forever.

❧

The next morning, Glenys woke to a new world. She laid in bed with her hands behind her head reliving the day before.

She relished the joy she felt for Trista and Vic, and she delighted in the feel of brushing Tim's arm when she sat next to him at church.

Vowing to make the best of her time there, she rose to get ready for another fun day. Today was a presentation for some visiting schools. She'd been branded The Owl Lady and didn't mind the moniker a bit. Using her performing skills, she took on the role of an overenthusiastic bird-watcher. She'd pretend to have stumbled upon the center with her binoculars in tow and "discover" the owls. Then she'd flip open a book and read out loud about each one. Apparently the kids loved to learn right along with her.

Before she could leave the house, however, her cell phone rang. It was her agent. "Great news!" Sidney always started out that way, whether it was great news or not. She would just spin it to make it sound good. "They've moved the audition up to this afternoon. Tony Farentino is going out of the country unexpectedly and wanted to have this part of the process finished. Be there at three o'clock."

Glenys's heart thudded to her feet. First of all, she still hadn't held a peregrine falcon. She was going to work on that in the next couple of days. Secondly, she hadn't told Sidney where she was. She figured she'd beat her fear of birds and be back before anyone knew she'd been gone. "Um. . .I'm kind of not in LA right now."

"So? Mash that gas pedal and get here pronto."

"I'm in Oregon."

Total silence on the phone. Had Sidney fainted? Finally she heard a strangled groan. "What are you doing there? No. Don't explain. Just listen. I'm going to get you a ticket. Where will you be flying out of?"

"Merrick, but—"

"Fine, get yourself to Merrick and pick up your ticket. I'll get you here if I have to fly the plane myself." A click ended their one-sided conversation.

Glenys sank onto the couch with her keys still in her hand. She glanced over to Jackie Jr. and her babies, who were just beginning to look like mice. She warred within herself, one part telling her to grab her bags and go. The other, however, reminded her of Tim. Of their first kiss. Of his excitement over her breakthrough as she held Heidi for the first time. Of their holy victory as they watched two arrogant people humble themselves before Christ. She thought of Gramps and dancing with him to an imaginary tune. And she thought of Cyrano, the first bird she'd ever wanted to get to know.

But her life was in Hollywood. Her dream was to have a major cinematic role. She couldn't abandon her desire.

She ran to Trista's room, threw open the door, and pounced on the sleeping lump in the middle of the bed. "Wake up! I need to talk! Now!"

Trista's saggy eyes focused slowly. "Okay." She pulled herself up to lean on her pillow and rubbed her face. "What?"

Glenys recounted what had just happened. "And she wants me to get to Merrick right away to catch the next plane back."

By the end of her tale, Trista was wide awake. She thrust the covers off the bed and started to head out the door. "What are you waiting for? Let's get you packed."

Glenys grabbed her arm. "But do I really want to go?"

This stopped Trista cold. "I know my dad, and if you blow this audition, he will never ask for you again."

"But I have obligations here. A school presentation today and Gramps's birthday this afternoon. I can't skip out on those."

Trista's demeanor changed. She patted Glenys's arm. "You know, the old me would pack for you, force you into the car, and toss you onto the plane. But I understand now that you need to pray." She smiled. "I can't be your lighthouse this time."

"Oh. That's just evil, throwing my own words back to me."

But Glenys realized that it was true: Trista had become her career mentor and phobia therapist. Having a good friend to bounce things off of was never a bad thing, but she'd leaned too hard on Trista, sometimes choosing her over God. "You're right. This is too big a decision to make quickly."

"Then my advice is to go to the audition, and if nothing comes of it, you'll know that wasn't what God wanted."

"I can always come back, right?"

"Right."

Even while she packed, she knew she'd upset people in Shady Pine. But she told herself she'd make up for it later. She couldn't disappoint Tim over the phone, however. So on her way to Merrick, she stopped at the center. She knew he'd be working in the morning since Gramps's birthday party was that afternoon.

Where was his car? Would she have to leave without the chance to say good-bye?

Mandy was just leaving the office in the visitor center as Glenys walked in. She stopped her to break the bad news. "They moved up my audition. I need to leave this morning, so I won't be able to be there for the kids."

The disappointment on Mandy's face tugged at Glenys's heart. "I'm so sorry to hear that. But we'll just give it the way we always have. Good luck. . .or break a leg."

She started to wander out the door when Glenys stopped her. "Where is Tim? I need to say good-bye."

"He's out picking up an injured osprey at Lost Creek Reservoir. You could try calling him."

Glenys sighed. If that was the only way she could talk to him, it would have to do. She punched in his number but only reached his voice mail. If he was doing a water rescue, he had probably thrown his cell phone into the glove compartment as he did at Crater Lake. She didn't leave a message, preferring to explain directly.

Glenys looked at her watch. No time to wait for him. Sidney had called while Glenys was on the way to the center to let her know the time and flight number. Maybe it was better to call Tim after all—from far away. Then she wouldn't have to see the disappointment on his face.

Alone for the last time with Cyrano, she walked over to his play area. He'd been unusually quiet, and she wondered if he was sick. "Hello?" She tried to coax him to talk. "Sweetheart?"

He lifted his wings in a quick flutter, then looked into her eyes. "Freckle."

"Honestly, Cyrano. You say the strangest things."

"Heart-shaped. . .freckle."

Her hand flew to her neck.

"Kiss. . .freckle."

Who knew about her freckle? She thought back. She rarely put her hair up because it never stayed. But she had pulled it off her neck the day she and Tim were looking for Gramps and she'd become overheated.

"Pretty. . .green eyes. . .dimple."

It was Tim saying those things about her.

"Oh, Cyrano. He does care." But she couldn't wait for him to let him know that she cared back. "If only I could be in two places at once. My home and career are calling me, but Tim has my heart."

All the way to Merrick and the airport, she questioned herself. But once she boarded the plane, she'd reached the point of no return. Hollywood or bust, and she feared it was Tim's heart that would ultimately be busted.

☙

Tim thanked the fisherman who had found the osprey flailing in the reservoir. They met at the marina where the man's boat floated near a dock. He was waiting for Tim in the parking area.

The leathery, timeworn fisherman introduced himself as

Ron. He explained that he had spotted what he thought was an osprey and snatched it out of the lake. "I had a Mylar emergency blanket, so I covered it to keep it warm."

"Thanks for doing that. You're lucky he didn't fight back. You could have lost a finger." Tim followed him to his boat.

"I got steel-mesh fishing gloves. Gotta protect these dainty hands, ya know." He snickered at his own joke. " 'Sides, that little fellow was so spent, I don't think he coulda nipped at me."

They reached the small skiff, and Tim hopped in. He peered under a silver blanket on the floor to see a juvenile osprey blinking back at him. Once again, he was filled with awe at God's creation, even down to the black raccoon mask that served to reduce the sun's glare on the water so the osprey could hunt effectively.

With his thick falconry gloves on, Tim reached under the blanket and wrapped his fingers around the slender body and wings. "There you go, little guy. We'll get you fixed up." A spot of blood on the bottom of the boat told him they were dealing with something more traumatic than a broken wing. Upon further inspection, he noticed that the tip of one wing had been completely severed.

"Oh no." He looked into Ron's concerned face. "I'll take him in, but he'll never return to the wild."

Ron took off his hat and scratched his head. "How can the tip of his wing just come off like that?"

Tim's eyes scanned the area. "Did you hear a gunshot? That could have done it."

Ron shook his head.

"If you hadn't been out in your boat today, this little guy might have drowned."

Ron dug a business card from his wallet. "Let me know if there's anything I can do."

The card indicated that Ron Fester was *The* Fishing Guy. Tours, instruction, and all things with a pole.

Tim pocketed the card and handed him one of his own. "Thanks. Feel free to call any time to check up on his progress. Just ask for the osprey named"—he peeked at the card—"Fester."

Ron's face lit up like a Fourth of July sparkler. "Thanks, man. I'll do that."

After loading the osprey into the back of his SUV, Tim waved at the man and started his vehicle, being sure to turn off the radio. His passenger didn't need rock and roll on top of a scary car ride.

He dropped Fester off at the vet, then fished his cell phone from the glove compartment and called Mandy to report. After relating what he learned about their new resident, he said, "Hey, remember I'm only doing a flyby to get Cyrano, and then I'm taking the afternoon off for my grandfather's birthday. You have people to do the feeding, right?"

"Yeah, no problem. And Tim?" Mandy's voice took on a concerned tone.

"What, Mandy? You have bad news, I can tell. Is it Lady?"

"No, it's Glenys."

"Glenys?" He nearly dropped his phone.

"She came by here looking for you. Just a minute." She paused to speak to someone who interrupted the extremely important and confusing phone conversation.

"What did she want? Come on, Mandy! This isn't the time to keep me hanging."

She had apparently taken the phone from her ear. After an eternity, she came back on. "Sorry, Tim. What was I saying?"

"Glenys? Came by to look for me?"

"Oh, right. Her agent called to say her audition had been moved up. She's probably already on a plane for LA."

"She left?" A huge hole appeared in his heart, as if someone had punched right through it.

"Yes, but she said she'd call after the audition."

"Nice."

"Excuse me? You're breaking up."

Truer words were never spoken. "Thanks, Mandy."

Breaking up. An already fragile relationship severed, like Fester's wing. Glenys was gone, and he didn't even ask her to stay.

❧

After retrieving Cyrano from the center, Tim entered his house. Gramps had invited a handful of his breakfast buddies, and they sat in the living room swapping war stories. Would they never tire of that?

He placed Cyrano on his perch, wondering what was going on inside the bird brain. All the way home he had rattled on about a "heart."

"Did you remember the ice cream?" Aunt Barb greeted him from the kitchen.

"Rocky Road!" Gramps bellowed from his easy chair.

Tim kissed the balding head as he handed the plastic grocery sack to his aunt. "They don't make any other kind, do they, Gramps?"

Gramps chuckled and smoothed his thin patch of hair. "Not for me. Is that girl coming?"

The hope on Gramps's face broke Tim's heart. "No, I'm afraid not."

Aunt Barb poked her head out the kitchen door. "Why not? Timmy, what did you do?"

Tim took a defensive stance in the middle of the house, Aunt Barb standing there with her hands on her hips and Gramps glaring at him from his chair.

"Why do you think I did something? Believe me, she did this all on her own. Mandy told me that she's left to go back home. They moved up her audition."

"So"—Aunt Barb now folded her arms—"she didn't really have a choice."

"Oh, she had a choice. She could have told them she'd made a commitment here. But she just walked out on me." He kicked at the couch.

"You?" Aunt Barb raised an eyebrow.

Tim only just realized how that sounded. "I mean us. The center. Gramps and his party."

"Mm-hmm." She disappeared back into the kitchen.

Tim swiped at the hair near his eyes.

Cyrano flapped and danced in the corner, repeating unceasingly, "Tim. . .heart."

Yes. Tim had a heart, and he opened it for an actress. Stupid! And now he probably would never see her again.

Aunt Barb came out of the kitchen with paper plates and plasticware. "Are you just going to sit there pouting?"

"No. What still needs to be done?"

"Call the girl."

"I mean for the party."

"The party is taken care of. Go call the girl." Her drill sergeant demeanor didn't allow for discussion.

Tim suddenly felt twelve again. "What do I say? Thanks for the memories?"

"Thank her for volunteering at the center. Tell her how proud you are that she conquered her fear. Then explain how much she'll be missed and that she's welcome back anytime."

"Anything else?" He hadn't seen this side of his aunt in a long time.

"Yes, you might tell her that you love her."

"What? I don't—"

"*Awk!* Tim! Heart! Care!" Cyrano hadn't shut up since they'd come home. And now he was picking up on the heightened conversation between Tim and his aunt.

"Rocky Road!" And now Gramps.

"Fine!" Tim admitted defeat. "I'll do it outside where it's quiet."

He slammed open the back door and marched out to the river where he punched in Glenys's cell numbers. He prayed she was still on the plane and had her phone off, but when she answered, he suddenly couldn't remember any of the things Aunt Barb had told him to say, except the last one, which he wasn't about to admit.

"Um. . .so. . ." *Brilliant, Vogel.* He ought to follow that up with, "Der. . .Uh. . ."

"I'm so sorry, Tim. They called this morning, and you couldn't be reached. Mandy said it wasn't a huge deal about the presentation, but I still feel bad. And I wouldn't have missed Gramps's party if this wasn't important. Please tell him I'll bring him something extra special."

A knot formed in Tim's gut. "Then, you plan on visiting?"

"Of course, as often as I can. . .if you're okay with that."

"Oh, sure." He heard the bitterness in his voice. "We're used to revolving doors around here. But they get rusty after a while of nonuse."

"What are you talking about?"

"I know your kind." *Shut up, Vogel.* "You make an appearance, put on an award-winning performance, then leave. You may think you'll be back often, but you won't. We are just a stop on the tour and easily canceled."

"Tim, I am not your mother."

"No, but you're just like her, aren't you? Career over family?"

"Just wait a minute. Are you saying you consider yourself family to me?"

This immediately stopped his tirade. He wasn't family. He was just some guy she'd met while working at the center. But the way she had infused herself into his life, becoming the daughter to Gramps that he'd always wanted and making Tim look forward to working late at the center so they could be together. . .yes, she had become family to him. But what was he to her?

"Look," he finally said, "it was nice while it lasted. I knew you would have to leave someday; I guess it just came as a shock that it happened so soon."

"It shocked me, too. I wasn't ready to leave."

He rubbed the tension from his neck as his anger abated. "Really?"

"I was having so much fun. I almost didn't get on the plane."

"Then why did you?"

"I kept laying out fleeces. 'God, if You don't want me on that plane, make me late to the airport.' I was right on time. 'God, if You don't want me to audition, don't let there be taxis available at LAX.' My agent sent a car. 'God, tie up traffic.' I'm almost there now with plenty of time to spare."

"So you felt like I do right now."

"Which is. . .?"

He kicked a rock into the river. "Like I'm in a void. We didn't get to say good-bye." And—fine, he'll admit it—he didn't get to tell her how he felt about her. He didn't ask her to stay.

"A void, yes. Or a vacuum, like I've been sucked into the machinery of Hollywood without any care to my feelings. Before I left for Oregon, I wanted this audition so badly I could taste it. Nothing else would've gotten me into the bird sanctuary. But while there, I think I found another purpose. I'm very confused because working at the center is as important to me right now as winning this role. I'm praying that God will tip the balance because I obviously can't be in two places."

It meant a lot to hear that she was confused. He'd never gotten that with his mother. She clearly chose her career over her family, no looking back.

"Thank you, Glenys." Tim wandered along the bank.

"For what?"

"For helping at the center." No, those were his aunt's words. "I mean, for your courage, your passion. Not everybody knows what they want in life, and you worked past a major obstacle. I admire that."

"Thanks. I admire you for the work you do, too." Her voice sounded thick with emotion.

"I'll pray for you, Glenys. That God shows you clearly the desire of your heart and that he'll make the path smooth to attain it." And, if He chose to keep her in Hollywood, that He would dull Tim's pain.

seventeen

Glenys closed her phone and slipped it back into her purse. From the backseat of the sedan, she watched Los Angeles breeze by. Palm trees, storefronts, restaurants. All a part of her three weeks ago, but now seemed foreign. She glanced up at the sky hoping to see a proud eagle, but knew she'd never see anything like that in her hometown.

Hometown.

Where was that exactly? Could just a few short weeks totally alter her life, her dreams?

She arrived to her audition in time, but her heart wasn't in it anymore. However, she'd promised Mr. Farentino. And if he wanted her that badly, she certainly couldn't keep him waiting.

She walked to the room her agent had told her to go to, and when she opened the door, she was shocked to see other women waiting to try out. Mr. Farentino had told her that even though he wanted her in the role, she'd still have to audition. He'd led her to believe she'd be the only one. He'd probably told each of the twenty women the same thing. Was Dad right? Was Trista's father following his own agenda? But that was the biz. Half-truths, half-promises. She'd been disillusioned before, but the desire had always kept her going. Now she sat in the room full of people, wishing she were at the bird center. However, she knew herself well enough to realize that if she'd stayed at the center, she'd have longed to be here.

Someone handed her the usual form to fill out, and she sat next to a blond beauty who didn't look a thing like the character for which she was trying out.

"Excuse me." She pulled Blondie's attention from the fashion magazine she was reading. "Are we all trying out for the falconer?"

Blondie snapped her gum. "The what?"

"The role of the woman who raises falcons."

Seriously? Didn't she do her research?

"Oh, yeah. All of us. Plus I heard there was another session earlier today. There's probably a good fifty of us out for that part." She perused Glenys in her travel clothes and went back to her magazine.

After waiting a good half hour for her name to be called, Glenys's phone rang. Caller ID showed it was Tim. Her heart sang. Was he calling to wish her well on her audition?

"Hi, Tim. We only talked a little while ago."

"I know. I called to ask you to pray."

Jolts of alarm shot through her. "What's wrong?"

"It's Gramps. He went to blow out his candles and had a major emphysema attack. We're rushing him to the emergency room."

"Oh no!" Several of the women turned to look at her as she rose and left the room. "Do you need me there?"

A brief silence was followed with, "No. Just pray."

She was about to do just that aloud when he said good-bye and hung up. So she silently entreated God to watch over Gramps and heal him. When she reentered the room, she sat back down next to Blondie and listened to the gum snapping to the rhythm of the accusations in her own head.

You should have stayed. You shouldn't have skipped out on Gramps. You should show Tim that not everyone in the acting profession is like his mother.

Then again, a more familiar voice intruded. *This is what you've always dreamed of. Forget the fifty women—if God wants you in this role, it's yours. You've paid your dues, and now it's time to redeem them.*

She fidgeted in her seat. How long had she wanted to be an actress? She had never gotten this far in the process before. A director asking for you by name, even if you had to audition with fifty others, was better than a casting call of hundreds.

How long had she loved Tim? Not to mention Gramps, Shady Pine, and the center. When she worked with the owls, she never felt more fulfilled, like she was making a difference. She closed her eyes, and Dunk's sweet face appeared. And then Tim's face with his shaggy hair brushing his brow.

Tim said he'd pray for the desire of her heart.

Finally, she felt the balance tip.

❧

Tim stood near Gramps as he lay on the hospital bed. He had been admitted and was breathing easier now that he'd received treatment and oxygen. His paper-thin flesh draped over the skeleton of what was once a strong, capable man. But now he seemed to be disappearing before Tim's eyes.

Gramps swiped at the nasal prongs in his nose as he awoke, and Tim stilled his hands. A nurse with graying streaks in her brown hair walked in at that moment and checked the drip going into his IV. "How are you doing, Mr. Vogel?" She spoke in a loud voice, as if all elderly men were deaf. "Are you comfortable?"

"No." He glared at her. "I can't move while tied down. I'm not a prisoner of war, you know." He pointed at the clip on his finger. "And what is this?" He started to remove it, but the nurse gently but firmly clamped her fingers around his wrist and took his pulse, effectively taking his mind off the clip.

The pulmonologist who had admitted Gramps to the hospital also stepped in and checked the chart at the foot of the bed. Without looking at Gramps, he made a notation in the chart and said, "We're going to keep you overnight and discuss options for your COPD tomorrow. I'll consult with your doctor, but be prepared to be set up with oxygen at home."

"Why, you whippersnapper." Gramps frowned and pointed his clipped finger at the doctor. "I'm writing up a letter of reprimand and sending it pronto to your commanding officer."

The doctor's lips twitched, and he raised an eyebrow. "Check his oxygen again," he said to the nurse. "He seems to be hallucinating."

Tim rubbed the back of his neck. "Actually, he's been having problems with that lately. He had an appointment to be seen for dementia, but these bouts of emphysema keep stalling it."

The doctor checked the records again. "That should be noted here." He scribbled in the chart. As he turned to leave, he saluted Gramps with a weak Boy Scout gesture, his only attempt thus far at acknowledging his patient beyond the chart.

"Don't you salute me." Gramps craned his neck from the pillow, looking like an eaglet bobbing its head. "I'm a non-com and your sergeant. Save it for someone who gets paid enough to care."

"Yes, sir." Although the doctor received no brownie points for his actions upon entering, Tim's estimation of the man rose a little as he backed out apologizing.

"That's Sarge to you!" Gramps bellowed from the bed.

The nurse fisted her hips. "Now see here. You're in my hospital now, soldier. While you're here I pull the rank, understand?"

Gramps's eyelids flew open, and he seemed to sink farther into his pillow. "Yes, ma'am."

She winked at Tim as she left the room. A moment later he heard the door open again behind him and assumed she had returned. But Gramps's face brightened. "Libby?"

Tim closed his eyes and breathed a prayer of thanks. So Glenys had come after all. "No Gramps, it's Gl—"

"Daddy!"

The woman swept into the room, her high-heeled open-toed shoes clicking on the floor and her chic purple scarf whipping him on her way by.

"Mom?"

"Oh, hi, Timmy." She air-kissed him on the cheek. "How is he? Barb called when they admitted him."

"How did you get here so fast? I just texted you an hour ago."

"I came in earlier today to see a friend perform at the Shakespeare Festival. He's starring in *Man of La Mancha* this evening. Since I was so close, it wasn't hard to hop in the rental and rush over."

It took less than a half hour to get from Oakley to Merrick. Tim doubted she immediately rushed out.

She checked her watch. "I'll need to leave in a little while."

"Of course. We wouldn't want you to miss your 'friend.'"

Her shoulder raised in a defensive move. "This guy may be the one. Can't you be happy for me?"

"So you'd come to Oregon to see a guy, but not your family."

"Tim." Aunt Barb had just entered the room and gave him a warning look as she motioned with her eyes to Gramps. Okay, no confrontations right now. But later, his mother, who frowned at his comment, would hear an earful.

She gazed at Gramps and plopped down on the bed, then swept her maroon nails through his thin white hair. "I'm so sorry I missed your birthday party, Daddy."

Tim controlled his gag reflex. What was her game?

Gramps sought Tim with his eyes. "Is this really Libby this time?"

"Yes, Gramps. It's Mom."

Pure joy beamed from his face. Tim had been wanting this moment for so long, but now that it was here, he couldn't keep the mixed emotions from overwhelming him. He left the room, bolting past his aunt.

❧

Glenys landed in Merrick. Two airplane rides in one day. Exhausted from the whirlwind she'd been caught in, she hopped into a cab and instructed the driver to take her to the Merrick Medical Center, where Gramps had been last time.

Her heart thumped so hard she could barely hear, but once she arrived, she quickly found the room and entered.

Gramps turned his gaze to her, then frowned. "Libby?" He then looked at the woman sitting on the bed next to him.

Glenys stopped short when she saw her. Not because she looked out of place with her black and purple Dior dress, but because in an eerie Botox way, she had a familiar face.

Glenys peered more closely. "Aunt Barb?"

The woman regarded her as if she were a fly that had just entered the room. "She's my twin. Who are you?"

"Are you Tim's mom?" Glenys couldn't stop staring.

"Daddy, do you know this person?"

Gramps furrowed his brow as if in concentration. Clearly confused, he finally said, "I don't know."

Aunt Barb entered the room just then. "Glenys! You came."

Glenys turned and gratefully accepted the matronly hug. "You're a twin!" She waved her hands in excitement. "This reminds me of when I was an extra in a show from the science fiction channel, *Leave Me AClone*. It was horrible."

Aunt Barb chuckled and turned to the beautiful, but hard-edged person guarding Gramps. "Libby, this is Glenys, Tim's friend. They met at the bird center."

Libby relaxed somewhat. "Well, if she's Timmy's friend. . ."

Glenys looked from one woman to the other. "I don't understand. If you two are twins, why does Gramps keep thinking I'm her?"

Libby bristled. "Oh please."

Aunt Barb continued to cradle Glenys's arm, offering comfort in this woman's wake. "I wondered that, too. He was never confused by me, and we're identical. Maybe it wasn't the look as much as the attitude. Libby used to be a young, sparkling starlet."

"Oh, and what am I now?" Libby thrust out her chin.

"A middle-aged actress."

Libby folded her arms in a pout. "I'm not middle-aged."

"My dear, we're the same age. If it weren't for plastic surgery, you would sag in as many places as I do."

Libby huffed.

Able to breathe now that this startling revelation had come and gone, Glenys asked, "Where's Tim? He didn't know I was coming."

Aunt Barb glanced toward the door. "He's been very restless, hardly staying in this room for more than a few minutes. I imagine he's wandering around out there somewhere."

Despite the gatekeeper, Glenys approached, and lifted Gramps's hand to her cheek. "I'm Glenys, remember? We've been to church together, ate some meals. I've hung out with you at the house?"

Clarity filtered into his red-rimmed eyes. "Oh. Timmy's girl."

She liked the sound of that. "I'm going to go find him, but I'll be right back. Okay?"

"Okay."

She kissed his hand and laid it back onto the sheets with care. Then, with much effort, she looked at Tim's mother. "Pleasure to meet you."

"Likewise." Tim's mom raised her nose in the air. Glenys suspected Libby didn't mean it any more than she.

Passing Aunt Barb, she reached for her hand and drew strength from her squeeze. Then she left the room in search of Tim.

eighteen

After leaving the hospital grounds entirely to get dinner for himself and Aunt Barb, Tim had cooled off somewhat. But he still wasn't sure he could handle his mother, regardless of the fact that he'd wanted her there. When he reentered the hospital room holding out the peace offering of a hamburger and lemon-lime soda, Aunt Barb accepted it gratefully.

"Thanks," she whispered. "The birthday cake wore off about an hour ago."

"For me, too. And I missed lunch when I picked up the osprey."

She glanced out the door, a weird grin on her face. "Did you happen to run into anybody on your way in?"

"No, why?"

"Oh, no reason. Someone was looking for you earlier, but I told them you'd be right back."

"Who?"

She waved away his question. "I'm sure it wasn't important. Let's eat this in the lounge so Dad won't want any." She darted out of the room. Perhaps the pressure of Gramps's illness was beginning to get to her.

His mom sat on the bed and had smiled at him when he came in. Guilt stabbed a bony finger into his chest. He hadn't thought to bring her anything.

"I'm sorry. Would you like me to run back out?"

She waved the offer away. "I'll be leaving soon."

He started to follow Aunt Barb out the door, but turned toward his mother. "Will you be coming back? After the play is over? How long will you be here?"

She stood and palmed his cheek and gazed into his eyes in the same way Aunt Barb always did, shocking him with the rare motherly moment. "You've grown to be an awesome person. Thank you for taking care of Gramps—my daddy." Were those genuine tears pooling in her eyes?

He noticed that she'd evaded his question, but what she did say began to heal the scar of her leaving. She'd never said thank you or acknowledged his dedication in any way.

All he could manage was a head nod. She kissed his cheek, then turned back to Gramps, who had been sleeping ever since Tim had gotten back. "He's so old."

Tim expected her to say something about her missing so much, but that never came.

She hugged herself and went back to her bedside vigil.

When Tim joined Aunt Barb in the visitor's lounge, he was shaking his head. She raised an eyebrow, and he answered her unspoken question. "Mom is acting as if she's sorry she's been gone for so long."

Aunt Barb opened the white paper bag and drew out the burgers and fries, setting them on the white side table. "I think she is, but she doesn't know how to become a part of our lives."

Tim sat next to her and took a bite of a cold french fry but put the other half back in the paper envelope it came in. Hunger had fled, and in its stead came the same guilt that had attacked him earlier. "Do you think we've been making it hard for her to return?"

Again, the eyebrow raised as she considered his words. "Could be. Dad has always been welcoming, but you and I probably make her feel uncomfortable." She picked at the bun of her hamburger. "Maybe we should pray about how to love her instead of attacking her choices."

Tim had to let that marinate a moment. "One of the choices had been to leave her five-year-old child."

"You know," Aunt Barb continued, "Libby regretted getting

pregnant when she was only eighteen, but the word *abortion* never crossed her lips. And giving you up, even for adoption, was out of the question."

"But—"

"Let me finish. I don't think anyone has ever explained this to you. Mom and Dad were supportive of her decision. She worked hard to get a performing arts degree, and by then the acting bug had bitten hard. She saw that she could do something she loved and still help support you. She sent home a portion of each paycheck for your care."

"I needed more than money, though. I needed a mom."

"I know, and if she'd been capable of those feelings, she would have stayed with you. But even she recognized that she hadn't been cut out to be a mother. The best thing she did for you was get out of the way so you could be raised properly."

Tim brooded about this information, training his eye on the pattern in the rug.

In his silence, Aunt Barb continued. "I want you to think about this," she said as she tapped the back of his hand. "She was an immature teenage mother, frightened to realize that she'd put herself in that position. The only way she could support you was to move away. She knew you were in excellent hands."

"Even so, I knew I was different growing up. On Mother's Day, I never knew what kind of card to buy. All of them gushed with sentiments like 'you were there for me' and 'my most wonderful memories were with you.' I watched my friends interact with their mothers and wanted so badly to be able to hug my mom instead of just telling her I loved her over the phone." He squeezed his fist so hard a knuckle cracked. "Being raised by two grandparents and an aunt and uncle was not the same as having a parent there."

"We did the best we could."

Tim glanced up. "I know. And I love you all for it."

She nodded, but her eyes suddenly shimmered with unshed moisture.

He suddenly felt an overwhelming love and appreciation for this woman and her own sacrifices and stood to draw her into a hug.

"You know how much I struggle with your mother, but don't be too hard on her," she said against his shoulder. "She will never be perfect. Your grandparents accepted that a long time ago. Instead they decided to concentrate their efforts into prayers for her salvation." She cleared her throat. "I think we need to do the same."

She will never be perfect. Those words jostled a recent memory. When he and Glenys went to Oakley for the play and then stopped at the alpaca ranch, the owner said something similar. *People have their faults. Only Jesus is perfect.* The woman—Hannie was it?—had done something even more horrendous than his mother. She had abandoned her child in a public park. Yet her son came to forgive her eventually.

His heart twisted at his own shortcoming. He'd always prayed that his mother would love him, want to be with him. But never had he prayed for God to help him love her, despite her actions—her imperfections.

Aunt Barb wrapped what was left of her hamburger and put it back in the bag. Then she patted his arm. "I'm going to go back to sit with Dad."

"I'll be there in a minute. I just need to be alone right now."

He leaned his elbows on his knees, his face in his palms. The room was empty now that night had fallen.

Lord, I can't forgive my mom on my own. As imperfect as she is, my shortcoming is in accepting who she is and loving her in spite of it. You have called us to love the unlovely. Help me to do that. Even if she never changes, never let me refuse to pray for her again. And remind me when needed that I'm not perfect either. I really blew it with Glenys, judging her before I got to know her.

And please, give me a second chance with her. Amen.

When he looked up, feeling lighter than he had in ages, he saw a vision, an answer to his prayer. Glenys stood in the doorway, looking as though not sure if she should approach.

"Are you real?" The words were goofy, but he had to say them. The lightness from his prayer turned into giddiness from this woman's presence. He popped out of the chair and hugged her, relishing the feel of this flesh-and-blood woman after asking God for a second chance.

"I saw you and Aunt Barb in here, and I didn't want to intrude."

"I'm so glad you came." He pulled away abruptly. "What about your audition?"

With her arms still wrapped around his neck, she laughed. "I didn't stay for it. But it doesn't matter. I'm where I belong now."

"Did they have a falcon there? You didn't leave running and screaming, did you? Not after all your progress?"

Her dimple deepened, and she waved the thought away. "No. I could have handled any bird they might have thrown at me. Except a vulture." She shuddered. "I left because I have a new passion. And a new reason to live it." She pointed at his chest. "You."

He stroked her red-brown hair. "I've loved you from the moment you ran away screaming that first day."

"I know."

"You know?"

"A little bird told me." Then she whispered, "Cyrano has loose lips."

"Well, he's a fine, feathered friend."

"Good thing, too, because you weren't talking." She tilted her head, and he lowered his for her kiss. When they parted, she chuckled while nuzzling his cheek. "Who knew I'd fall for a bird guy?"

He swallowed the lump in his throat. "Who knew I'd fall for an actress?"

She narrowed her eyes. "Hmm, let's say actress on hiatus. I've put my career on hold until I figure out what I really want to do. And right now, I like performing little bird books at the center."

"Then you're here to stay?"

She nodded, and he claimed her lips once more.

epilogue

"You've been here eleven months. It's time to go."

Tim's words created a sweet pain in Glenys's heart. If she could trust her sorrow-filled throat, she also felt the need to say something. "It's been life-changing getting to know you." A half-sob escaped her throat. "If it weren't for you, I'd never have gotten over my fear."

They both stood on the Cleetwood Cove dock at Crater Lake saying good-bye to Lady, the once-feared but now much-loved peregrine falcon.

Mandy and Camille, along with Ethan and a slew of people from the community, pressed in. All of them had been more than willing to brave the steep hike down to Crater Lake.

"We have to do it, Tim." Mandy placed a hand on Tim's arm. "It's always hard releasing a bird we've come to love." She glanced at Glenys. "And I know it's especially hard for you."

Yes, Lady of the Lake had frightened her. But now she stood with Lady on her fist, confidant of her falconer skills.

Tim faced the crowd. "Thanks for coming everyone."

They all, about twenty-five people, whisper-clapped as they had been taught, enthusiastically showing their support for Lady, but making little noise so as not to spook her.

"You have all been important supporters for Lady's success," he continued. "From the monetary to the hands-on, it was all needed to put this magnificent creature back where she belongs."

Everyone grinned back, Ethan's smile especially broad. He had eagerly volunteered his time, taking care of Lady and learning all the ins and outs of the center. And now he wore the Shady Pine Raptor Center emblem on his shirt.

"Lady had a tough go of it. Several infections and that scare when we thought she might lose a part of her wing." Tim's voice cracked. "But through your love and prayers, she rallied. She became the star attraction at the flight enclosure as she made breakthrough after breakthrough, learning to fly again and to hunt."

Glenys remembered fighting not to scream and run as she watched the predator stalk an innocent mouse. But she had hung in there, gripping Tim's hand until he winced. That part of the process still stirred emotion, but she knew it was an important part of the raptor rehab process.

Tim glanced at her. "Ready?"

She nodded, feeling like a mother watching her daughter walk down the aisle and away from the nest. "Let's do it."

Lady of the Lake tilted her head as her sharp eyes caught every movement beyond her grasp. She had been banded so they could keep tabs on her, but other than that, she looked like the free bird God had intended when He created her.

Glenys breathed a prayer. "Lord, please keep Lady safe out there. Fly with her."

She cast her arm upward. Lady thrust her wings out and leaped, soaring overhead as if saluting with her wings one last good-bye.

Her victory screech as she disappeared across the lake and out to the island finalized not only her rehab, but Glenys's as well. Lady's freedom had become Glenys's freedom, and her heart soared with the falcon in thanks to a loving God who would not leave her, nor forsake her.

&

"I can do this." Glenys spoke to Trista on her cell phone a month after Lady of the Lake's release. She was in the car, meeting Tim at a middle school for a presentation. She had settled into her own rented home in Shady Pine, but once in a while still needed to connect with her friend. "I've spent one winter here and am looking forward to the next. This California girl is where she belongs."

In fact, Glenys had endured winter at the center surprisingly well. Despite the cold and snow, her heart warmed at working side by side with Tim.

"So, you're fitting in there. Who knew you'd become a bird person?"

"They've given me a title. I'm their first ever Production Manager. I get to work with the education department to write, direct, and usually star in plays featuring a cast of predatory birds. And Cyrano gets into the act often, hamming it up."

"I'm so happy that you're happy." Trista sighed. "Is your dad still bugging you about becoming a lawyer?"

"No, he knows that will never happen. After he visited me at Christmas, he could see my contentment. And miracle of all miracles, he got along with Tim."

"What about Tim's mom? She on board with you two as a couple?"

"She's the same. All about her career. She doesn't care who Tim dates. But she's making more of an effort to stay in touch."

"I'm sure you're praying for her."

"Every day."

"Keep the faith. If God can save me, he can save anybody."

Glenys took a moment to thank God for his faithfulness. "So, how are you?"

"I'm veh-rry happy." She dragged out *very* until she almost purred.

"I never thought I'd miss Vic. How is he doing in his new job?"

"Great. The LA Zoo is a good fit for him. He's really enjoying working in the California Condor Rescue Zone."

Glenys shuddered. Condors were too close to vultures.

"Hey, Tris, I'm looking forward to visiting next spring for the wedding. Have you decided on my maid of honor dress?"

"I'm thinking something with tons of ruffles. . .maybe orange."

Glenys laughed. "I know you better than that." She remembered the sweet time when Vic and Trista both accepted Christ into their lives. They would be starting their new life with a firm foundation, and this brought tears of joy to Glenys's eyes.

The school came into view, and she pulled into the parking lot. "I'm here. Gotta go. Give Vic a hug from me, okay?"

Tim met her at his SUV, and after a quick kiss, she helped carry the birds needed for the presentation into the middle school.

She had written the near-autobiographical story "Miss Hoot Learns to Love." After donning a dowdy costume, Glenys threw herself into character for the role of Miss Hoot, a person frightened of birds until a little owl named Dunk stole her heart. Throughout the play, her costume changed from colorless to colorful with clever tricks. A gray hat turned inside out became bright yellow with a red ribbon. Her plain sweater became orange dotted with daisies in the same manner. The ankle-length skirt converted when she pulled up one corner and buttoned it to the side, revealing feminine purple petticoat ruffles. In the end, Miss Hoot's gray, fearful world became full of happy colors.

As she delivered her last line in the small assembly, thanking Dunk on his perch for helping her see that all birds have a place and need not be feared, a gray feathered flurry caught her eye. Cyrano flew in and landed on her hand.

Surprised to see him there when he wasn't in this story, she asked, "What's this?" Something shiny hung from his beak. She held out her palm, and he dropped a gold ring with a solitary diamond into it.

"*Awk.* Marry us."

On cue, Tim walked across the stage, plucked the ring from her hand, and bent on one knee. Then, holding the ring out to her, he said, "Please."

Joy like she'd never known bubbled from her like the headwaters of the Rogue River. "Yes. Of course!"

He slipped the ring onto her finger, then stood and glanced into the audience of kids where Gramps and Aunt Barb stood at the back, smiling. "She said yes!"

While the kids all groaned their corporate *E-e-e-w*, Glenys suddenly found herself swept into his hug, happy kisses preempting her breathing. Cyrano had moved to Tim's shoulder and became the official announcer.

"*Awk!* Pretty green eyes. . . dimples. . .heart-shaped freckle. . . care. . . Yes! Yes! Of course!"

Dear Reader,

This story was about fear. A subject I'm sure we can all identify with. Glenys had a severe case of ornithophobia, a fear of birds. It debilitated her to the point of getting in the way of her dream.

Fear comes in all degrees. I used to fear the dark when I was a child. But that fear slowly diminished over the years. Now I have no trouble walking through the house at night. However, I've developed a fear of stepping on something the cat left behind. Perhaps that fear isn't as irrational as others.

When I was researching this book, Brian, the bird handler at Cascades Raptor Center in Eugene, Oregon, showed me the Breeder Barn. I have a thing about mice. Not a jump-on-the-chair-and-scream type of fear (well, maybe a little), but a sickening, "I remember the smell from when my house was infested that one year" type of fear. As he spoke, his words sounded as though they came from deep inside a cavern. I don't know what he told me in that cramped shed. I just knew I had to get out in the fresh air.

Do you have a fear that is ruining your life? Is it something you can face head-on as Glenys did, or is it more subtle, such as a fear of a memory—as was my mouse experience?

Whatever your fear, God wants to replace it with a "spirit of power, of love and of self-discipline" (2 Timothy 1:7). Glenys repeated to herself, "I can do everything through him who gives me strength" (Philippians 4:13). That verse may often be said in a flippant manner, but look deep into its truth. Only through Christ can you find strength. If you are fighting a fear, don't look within yourself, but look to the Lord. He is the only one who can give you the power to overcome.

Blessings,
Kathleen

A Letter To Our Readers

Dear Reader:

In order that we might better contribute to your reading enjoyment, we would appreciate your taking a few minutes to respond to the following questions. We welcome your comments and read each form and letter we receive. When completed, please return to the following:

Fiction Editor
Heartsong Presents
PO Box 719
Uhrichsville, Ohio 44683

1. Did you enjoy reading *Fine, Feathered Friend* by Kathleen E. Kovach?
   ❏ Very much! I would like to see more books by this author!
   ❏ Moderately. I would have enjoyed it more if

   _____

   _____

   _____

2. Are you a member of **Heartsong Presents**? ❏ Yes ❏ No
   If no, where did you purchase this book? _____

   _____

3. How would you rate, on a scale from 1 (poor) to 5 (superior), the cover design? _____

4. On a scale from 1 (poor) to 10 (superior), please rate the following elements.

   ____ Heroine   ____ Plot
   ____ Hero   ____ Inspirational theme
   ____ Setting   ____ Secondary characters

5. These characters were special because? _____
_____
_____

6. How has this book inspired your life? _____
_____
_____

7. What settings would you like to see covered in future
   Heartsong Presents books? _____
_____
_____

8. What are some inspirational themes you would like to see
   treated in future books? _____
_____
_____

9. Would you be interested in reading other **Heartsong
   Presents** titles? ❏ Yes ❏ No

10. Please check your age range:
    ❏ Under 18   ❏ 18-24
    ❏ 25-34   ❏ 35-45
    ❏ 46-55   ❏ Over 55

Name _____
Occupation _____
Address _____
City, State, Zip_____
E-mail _____

NIGHTSHADE

They've championed freedom, survived the cruelties of war, and now these same heroes return home. . .wounded and discarded. Former Navy SEAL Max Jacobs is unable to control his anger and alienates himself from his wife, who files a protective order against him. Their lives are about to collide when Sydney Jacobs hunts down the source of a human interest story at her local newspaper. Will she uncover Nightshade, the elite team Max is covertly working with, and bring danger both to Max and herself.

Contemporary, paperback, 368 pages, 5½" x 8⅜"